CW00552262

Praise for Dan and Robert Zangari

"Dan Zangari and Robert Zangari have crafted a superb opening epic to what promises to be a deeply involved and dedicated fantasy series."

—K.C. Finn, Readers' Favorite

"Absolutely fantastic! [In *A Prince's Errand*] you get those hints of the *Wheel of Time*—that huge epic scale Robert Jordan really tried to produce. You get that sense of majesty with the books that Brandon Sanderson writes. There is a gritty realism to it with something like Robert E. Howard, with threads of David Eddings... [*A Prince's Errand*] is a beautiful, beautiful piece of passion. If you're looking to pick up a book that will keep you hooked for a long, long time, make sure to get this book."

—Cameron Day, Comics, Clerics, & Controllers

"*A Prince's Errand* is an intricately crafted tale of high fantasy that is as rich in detail as it is in entertainment."

—Michael Cole, Design Wizard Blog: Top 50 Wattpad Books of 2018

.

BY **DAN ZANGARI & ROBERT ZANGARI**
PUBLISHED BY LOK PUBLISHING

DAN ZANGARI & ROBERT ZANGARI

A THIEF'S WAY

Companion Story One of TALES OF THE AMULET

LOK
PUBLISHING

A LOK PUBLISHING BOOK · SALT LAKE CITY

LEGENDS OF KALDA®

Tales of the Amulet

A THIEF'S WAY

Hardcover Edition

Copyright ©2019 Dan Zangari & Robert Zangari
All rights reserved.

Made in the U.S.A.

Cover Art by Kerem Beyit
Chapter Heading Illustrations by Suleyman Temiz
Cartography by Robert Zangari

Edited by Linda Branam

First Printing: October 5th, 2020
First Paperback Edition: October 5th, 2020

ISBN 10-digit: 1-947673-15-7

ISBN 13- digit: 978-1-947673-15-1

Visit our web site at www.legendsofkalda.com

CONTENTS

CARDA WASTES
(Terrain Unknown)

Bradisar

THE BLACK MOUNTAINS

Duras

COMDOLITH

Crimdor

Ihen Valley

Cordan

Kardorth

Karthar

MALTIN

THE ELVEN REALM

CORDATH

Mitorn

Merath

(Topography Estimated)

New Sorjin

KILDATH

LITOR

Kildath

Litlim

SEA OF
KORATH

TILSANA GULF

LOSIAN GULF

TURBULANT SEA

KALADORN

KERINDOR

Los

Estrom

Kerlaris

Alath

GASTRIM

KINGDOM OF LOS

Gastrim

Arbath

WESTERN SOVEREIGNTY

HENDEN

Tor

Monddar

Henden

MELAR FOREST

MINDOLARN EMPIRE

KLIS

Klath

Mindolarn

Klis

ALGIN GULF

Korum

Hilarn

HOLORUM

DENDEM ISLES

KALISHIR OCEAN

ISLE OF
MERDAN

CART..

Keth

CANTIR ISLES

NEMDAR ISLANDS

PRINCIPALITY OF SOROTH

Soroth

UNITED ISLES OF DAMNIR

The V

ISLE OF

KALDA

CIRCA 6,793 C.D.

10 20 30 40 50 60 70 80 90 100
Length in Hundred Grand Phineals

ABODINE
WASTELAN

Nyesil

THE FORSAKEN LANDS OF
AZRIN'IL

Xilarim   Osivir
DALISIN
CONFEDERACY

DESERT OF
ASH

Dalistim

SILRLAIN OCEAN

OCEAN OF TEMPESTS

Veir   Bithar
ACHEYLON

Arithan

IGEACEAN SEA

RUINED KINGDOMS OF
KRESH'DAL

THE FORBIDDEN LANDS

DESOLATE LANDS

SEA OF SAND

PEGALIC SEA

The musky smell of Orchin's Tavern disgusted Chernil. Putrid body odor—mixed with the stench of cheap alcohol—assaulted his nostrils as he scanned the crowded room. Puffs of lavin smoke occasionally filled the air. Uncouth men and women laughed raucous like the crass filth they were.

Why would a man of such notoriety choose a place like this *to socialize?* Chernil thought. The tavern was unbecoming of any who had even a measure of social prestige.

Perhaps I should have sent someone in my stead... But no, he reassured himself, *I need to meet him myself. This task is too important.* Demitru had insisted to Chernil that his friend was the best thief in all the civilized world—not to mention, he possessed some unique tevisrals. Even so, Chernil was still leery of hiring a man he had never met.

A whiff of cheap lavin wafted past Chernil's face, and he coughed in revulsion as he neared a barred window—the tavern's cashier booth. A dozing clerk sat behind the bars.

"Are you being paid to nap?" Chernil snarled.

The clerk started, flashing Chernil a glance with wide
eyes. "Oh, I'm sorry, sir. Cashing in? Or depositing?"

Chernil raised an eyebrow, and his snarl became more
pronounced. The clerk flinched. "I am looking for someone," Chernil said. "I have been told he frequents this
place."

The clerk looked about nervously and then leaned toward the bars. "You a plainclothes Watchman?" he whispered. "Or… a bounty hunter?"

Chernil set his jaw, and raised an eyebrow. Were bounty
hunters common in Soroth? "No, I am neither," he answered impatiently.

The clerk relaxed.

"His name is Tilthan," Chernil said. "Do you know
him?"

Laughing, the clerk nodded. "I sure do! In fact, he's sitting over there." He pointed across the tavern. "Second
table from the wall, middle row."

Chernil turned in the direction of the clerk's gesture,
eyeing the aforementioned table. Eight men sat around it
playing a card game. Half of them seemed to know each
other, as they were rowdily conversing. Though Chernil
couldn't hear them above the noise in the tavern, he deduced they were bantering with each other.

"Tilthan is the one with his back to the wall," the clerk
said. "The short one with the mole on his cheek. He's often in the company of that tall, chiseled fellow sitting to
his left. Nordal."

Chernil focused on Tilthan. He had an irreverent air
about him. The thin thief wore a wine-colored velvet doublet. He looked out of place in this crowd—a tad over-

dressed when compared to the other patrons. Tilthan rubbed at his mole, then ran his fingers through his neatly cropped brown hair, nervously eyeing the others at the table.

The other gamblers showed their cards, and Chernil deduced they were playing a game of Sharzen.

Suddenly, Tilthan's brown eyes flashed with excitement, and he violently stood, cheering. His abrupt movement knocked over his chair.

Chernil narrowed his eyes at Tilthan. *So, this is your friend, Demitru?* Compared with Demitru's refinement, Tilthan's untamed demeanor was stark.

"Is there anything else I can help you with?" the clerk asked.

"No," Chernil said curtly and moved toward the table, watching Tilthan rake in the polished spheres used as the tavern's chips.

"You're welcome!" the clerk muttered.

With all his sphere-chips gathered, Tilthan began a celebratory dance. Some of the gamblers at the table grimaced in frustration. The man identified by the clerk as Nordal chuckled, sitting back in his chair. He gave Tilthan an amused glance. One of the other, shorter men—sitting two places away on Tilthan's right—shook his head at the dancing thief and rolled his eyes.

One of your associates, Tilthan? Demitru had said that Tilthan worked with three others: two men, named Nath and Nemral, and a woman named Sharon. Together, they comprised a skilled thieving troupe.

"See, Nemral," Tilthan said in a gloating tone, "that's how it's done."

The man directly to the right of Tilthan's place nodded. Nemral was a little heavier than Tilthan, but his build was more muscular than pudgy. His face was pale, sprinkled with freckles, and wavy black hair adorned his head. He looked of Eastern Losian descent, especially with his vibrant blue eyes.

Losians, Chernil thought, disgusted. The mere thought of that accursed kingdom was more revolting than the tavern. It had been seven months since the massacre, but the horrific slaughter at the Feast of Sorrows was still fresh in his mind.

"I don't suppose you're interested in another game?" asked one of the men at the table. He had a prominent scar on his face.

"I'm afraid this game is finished," Chernil said, stopping at the table.

Tilthan abruptly stopped bragging and stared wide-eyed at Chernil.

"And who in Heleron's name do you think you are?" the scar-faced man demanded, his voice harsh.

"Yeah…" Tilthan said warily. "I'd like to know the answer to that, too."

Chernil gave the scar-faced man a glare, and then turned to Tilthan. "A mutual friend suggested I seek out you and your troupe," Chernil said. "I have a job for you."

Tilthan placed his hands on his hips. "What friend?" His tone was cautious.

Chernil glanced about the table. All eyes were on him. "Demitru."

The other man—who Chernil supposed was Nath—perked up, looking to Tilthan with an intrigued expression.

"Really...?" Tilthan said doubtfully. "And what does this *job* entail?"

"I would rather not speak of it here," Chernil said, his disgust for the tavern reflected in his tone.

Tilthan snickered, shaking his head.

What an irritating fellow, Chernil thought, drawing his lips into a line.

"So, you want to hire us?" Tilthan said, arching his eyebrows. "Well, we're not cheap." he said sardonically.

Chernil had expected as much. Lips pursed, he pulled a fist-sized sack from his belt and threw it at Tilthan. Its contents clinked as the thief caught it. "And there's more aboard my ship," he said.

Tilthan immediately opened the bag, and his eyes widened with greed.

Now I have you, Chernil thought. Demitru had told him how to properly persuade Tilthan. He had learned from Demitru that Tilthan often embarked on adventures, and he always sought gemstones in his share of the loot.

The other thieves and Nordal quickly gathered around Tilthan, each peering into the sack with surprise.

Chernil noticed the scar-faced man leaning forward, his eyes fixed on the spheres atop the table at Tilthan's place. The man's hand eased forward.

"You might want to cash in your spheres," Chernil suggested, jerking his head toward the table.

Tilthan shot a glance to the tabletop, seeing his former opponent reaching for the sphere-chips. "Oh... no you don't!" Tilthan jumped past his toppled chair toward the would-be thief.

The scar-faced man shot to his feet and departed empty-handed. The other card players followed him, leaving Chernil alone with Tilthan and his friends.

"What do you say, Tilthan?" Chernil asked. "I can pay each of you ten times what is in that sack."

Nath and Nemral turned to Chernil with slack jaws, their tongues almost hanging out of their mouths.

Nordal snorted. "Count me in, too!"

"No," Chernil said. "Just them. The task ahead requires a fair amount of stealth."

Nordal frowned.

"That's what we do best," Tilthan said, and grinned. He turned to the other two thieves. "Well, boys, what do you think?"

Nath gave Tilthan an annoyed gaze. "I think the answer is obvious, Tilthan," he said.

"You will be gone for several months," Chernil said, volunteering only the information he deemed necessary.

"Count us in!" Tilthan chimed. He removed an empty sack from the pocket of his velvet pants and began shoveling spheres into the sack.

"Good," Chernil said, "and how soon can you fetch your other associate?"

"Sharon?" Tilthan asked, looking up from the table.

"Uh, Tilthan," Nath interjected. "Ordreth is proposing to Sharon in two days... I suggest we don't involve her."

"Really?" Nordal asked, sounding surprised. "He's *actually* doing it?"

"Yeah..." Nath said. "But don't say anything. No one is supposed to know. I don't even think he's told Cornar, yet."

Nordal and Nath continued conversing about the proposal while Tilthan considered his friend's warning.

"She might not take kindly to us leaving her out," Tilthan finally said, squinting his eyes.

"I'm sure if we give her some of the payment it will ease her… uh…" Nath fumbled, "*disappointment.*"

Tilthan gave his friend a blank look. "Not from my share."

Nath rolled his eyes.

I can do with three, Chernil thought. Three thieves instead of four would not make the job impossible. *Perhaps it might even be more favorable this way.* At the very least, he wouldn't have to pay as much—not that it mattered. Wealth was not a stranger to Chernil.

Tilthan finished scooping up his winnings, then heaved the sack over his shoulder. It wasn't large enough to warrant such heaving. The gesture seemed ostentatious.

"Let me cash this in," Tilthan said.

Chernil nodded, stepping aside. "I will wait outside for you. But time is of the essence. We must set sail tonight."

Tilthan flinched.

"Do we have time to prepare for the trip?" Nath asked. "We need *some things*, if you know what I mean."

Chernil nodded, knowing the thief referred to their tevisrals. They would need those.

Nath hurried past Tilthan, moving toward the tavern's entrance.

"You can have my winnings," Nemral said to Nordal, leaving the table.

Nordal nodded his thanks, then looked to Chernil. "Are you sure you don't want me? I *am* a skilled warrior."

"I have my own bodyguards," Chernil said tersely, then

spun around. The sooner he could leave this grimy den, the better.

Outside in the fresh air, he took in a deep breath, relieved to be away from the filth of humanity. A moment later, Tilthan exited the tavern with Nath.

"*Now* can you tell us what exactly this job entails?" Tilthan asked. "I like to know *what* I'm stealing."

Chernil glanced over his shoulder, quickly scanning the street.

"Or at least where we're going..." Tilthan pried.

Satisfied that no one else was in earshot, Chernil lowered his voice to a whisper. "We're going to Korath. A Korathi noble unearthed a discovery several months ago, a relic from the time of the Karthar Empire. It—"

Tilthan groaned. "A relic... how dull."

Chernil stifled a rebuke and took a deep breath. *Such an insolent fellow*, he thought. "This is not just any relic," he said. He was about to continue, but a pair of footsteps sounded from a nearby alley. "We will speak further aboard my ship. It's docked at Pier Three, Wharf Twelve. Meet me there after you gather your belongings."

1

KORATH

I know you will not agree—none of our kind have through-out the ages—but you must be convinced! Destroying it will ensure that our Enemy never escapes his prison.

TWO MONTHS LATER

Tilthan was bored, tired of sailing. Not that he hated sailing. He rather enjoyed it. But the *amount* of sailing was another matter. Tilthan was accustomed to traveling aboard swift vessels, like the *White Duchess*. Captain Kenard's ship was one of the fastest in the entire world, traveling almost twice as fast as any other vessel. Tilthan supposed tevisrals were responsible for the increased speed, but Kenard never revealed his secrets.

Smart man.

Tilthan sighed as he leaned over the portside rail of the *Regalleon*—one of the ferries that traversed the landlocked Sea of Korath.

They had traveled on three ships since leaving Soroth:

Chernil's vessel, the ferry down the Gorbian River to the eastern banks of the Sea of Korath—and now the ferry to Korath itself. There had been a slight break in the sea travel, but it only lasted two days.

"Are we there yet?" he grumbled beneath his breath, hanging his head over the rail.

"I thought you would have asked that sooner," Nath said with a chuckle. "Judging by the position of the sun, we're only halfway between Gorbian and Korath."

Tilthan turned toward his thieving companion, giving him a blank stare.

Nath had a wide grin on his face, his arms folded. Tilthan enjoyed the occasional fun-filled banter, but sometimes Nath could be downright annoying.

Now was one of those times.

"I'm getting anxious, too," Nemral said with a sigh. "Two months of nothing…" He sat on the decking beside Tilthan, his head leaning against the rail.

Both Nath and Nemral were short men, like Tilthan. Their lack of height proved rather advantageous for their line of work. Tilthan couldn't count the number of times their smaller stature came in handy—well, him and Nath. Nemral was a little bigger, but he was no less agile.

"Just remember the gems," Nath said, his hazel eyes glancing between Tilthan and Nemral. He took in a deep breath and shook out his wavy light-brown hair. "I for one am enjoying the trip. I've never traveled this way to Korath."

"Hmph!" Tilthan huffed in exasperation.

"It's been some time since I visited Korath," Nemral said. "I came with Ginalia."

"Wow, that was a long time ago," Nath said.

"Yeah"— Nemral chuckled—"over ten years. Maybe twelve or thirteen…" He looked skyward, recounting the past. "It was a good trip. The weather was nice. The beaches were crowded, though."

"We were here a couple years ago," Nath said, "but we sailed from Kildath to Karbenath. I liked Karbenath."

"That was after your last adventure with Iltar and Cornar, right?" Nemral asked.

"Yup," Tilthan said. "Four years ago."

"Four years?" Nath asked, raising an eyebrow at Tilthan. "Uh, more like two."

"Whatever," Tilthan waved his hand airily. It felt like four years. He hardly saw anyone from the adventuring gang, besides Nordal and a few of Cornar's warriors. He had run into Iltar a few times, but it was just in passing.

I wonder when we're gonna go on another adventure, he thought. Tilthan had made his living on those adventures. Over the last eighteen years he had traveled the world with Iltar and Cornar, unearthing ruin after ruin. It was quite profitable.

Tilthan's great-uncle, Cedath, was a regular of Iltar and Cornar's adventuring band—well, technically someone other than Iltar and Cornar started it, but Tilthan couldn't remember who. Anyway, when Uncle Cedath's companions died on an adventure, he passed their thieving tevisrals to Tilthan. That day was one of the brightest amid those dark times.

Tilthan and his four closest friends had been about to go drinking when Uncle Cedath *appeared* within Tilthan's meager apartment in Klath—the southernmost port of the Kingdom of Los. It was the offer of a lifetime, his uncle had claimed. Uncle Cedath knew of Tilthan's desires to join the League of Surveillors, and also knew of his rejected application. Cedath's invitation, however, was meant to kindle the life Tilthan had yearned for since childhood.

And it did just that.

Uncle Cedath had three sets of thieving tevisrals. Tilthan of course claimed a pair for himself, but that left two pairs to split between his four friends. Kadren politely declined. Though the five of them had all wanted the life of intrigue and espionage, Kadren had become first mate on his father's shipping vessel, the *Eastern Spirit*. That was enough adventure for him.

That left Nath, Nemral, and Demitru.

Since Tilthan couldn't decide, they drew lots. Nath and Demitru won. Nemral was disappointed, though he tried not to show it.

Uncle Cedath took Tilthan and Nath under his tutelage, but Demitru went his own way. They had barely seen each other since then, which pained Tilthan.

But thinking of Demitru spurred his curiosity.

"Why would Chernil hire us instead of Demitru?" he asked, interrupting a conversation between Nath and Nemral.

"Because he needs more than just *one*?" Nemral said, his tone cryptic.

Nath nodded thoughtfully. "I've wondered the same thing…"

"Well," Nemral said with a grunt, "whatever the reason, I'm just happy to finally have a job."

Nemral hadn't been a part of the thieving troupe for very long. After their last adventure with Cornar and Iltar,

Uncle Cedath retired. He sold his tevisrals to Nemral. Perhaps *sold* wasn't the right word. Men usually had to sell kingdoms to obtain such tevisrals. Uncle Cedath had an arrangement with Nemral that was quite profitable. For every adventure or job Nemral undertook, he would have to pay Uncle Cedath one half of his earnings.

It wasn't a bad deal, all things considered. Most adventures yielded enough profit to live on for a decade.

Tilthan eyed Nemral, regretting that he hadn't chosen the man outright all those years ago.

The rest of the day on the ferry was uneventful and boring. Not even their games of Sharzen were enjoyable—what with only three players and tiny wagers. The ferry finally neared the large Isle of Korath, but they still had to sail to the island's capitol.

It was sunset when the city finally came into view.

Tilthan stood at the starboard bow with his thieving compatriots, eyeing the white sandy beaches around the city.

"I expected to see more people on the beach," Nemral said, frowning.

"It is kind of sparse," Nath remarked. "I wonder why."

Fall was upon the northern hemisphere of Kalda, but the cooler temperatures didn't seem to touch the Isle of Korath, which was known for its year-round warmth. Wealthy people from across the world often wintered in Korath, an ideal resort. Tourists came at all times of the year to bask on the beach.

The landscape upon which the city stood was a mix between white sandy beaches and rocky cliffs. Korath—the city—rose along cliffs and steep hills, spreading far inland.

Situated near the center of the city and atop the highest cliffs was the Korathi Palace. It overlooked the lower parts of the city, including the docking district. The palace's domed structures towered high, seeming higher than most Tilthan had seen. A wall surrounded the palace, except for along the cliffs. The steep cliffs were probably enough protection.

The *Regalleon* moored not long after reaching Korath. Tilthan and his companions were the first passengers to disembark. They hurried down the pier, carrying full sacks of their belongings—including their thieving tevisrals, which were well hidden.

As they neared the end of the pier, two men clad in plate armor approached, motioning for them to stop.

"Uh-oh…" Tilthan muttered. He hadn't remembered encountering the city's border patrol this close to the piers.

"Perhaps we should have snuck off the ship," Nath whispered.

Tilthan abruptly shushed his fellow thief, then straightened into a bold posture.

"You look ridiculous," Nath snickered.

Tilthan fought giving Nath a sharp glance.

"Good evening," one of the armored men said. Though their armor bore no insignia, Tilthan knew they were members of the City Watch.

"Evening," Tilthan said with a nod.

"Are you citizens or tourists?" the guardsman asked.

"Tourists," Nath said casually. "Why? What's the matter?"

By that time, more of the ferry's passengers neared Tilthan and the others. They crowded around the thieves, eyeing the guardsmen with confusion.

"Korath is not safe," the guardsman said. "Several murderers are loose within the city. Many have died. The widespread murders have also given rise to more crime, as our Watchmen are busy investigating each murder scene."

Unsettled gasps rippled through the crowd.

"We urge you to return to the ferry, for your own safety," the guardsman continued. "But, we will not stop anyone who still desires to enter Korath."

Worried conversations buzzed around Tilthan. A few of the ferry's passengers, however, continued down the pier, undaunted by the warning.

Tilthan feigned a cautious expression and turned to Nath. His fellow thief shrugged with open palms.

"I'm willing to risk it," Nath said.

"The beaches are safe, aren't they?" Nemral asked.

The guard didn't reply.

That didn't bode well.

Sighing, Tilthan noticed Chernil in the crowd with his bodyguards. They had agreed not to travel together. Chernil wanted to appear aloof from Tilthan and his troupe—an extra measure of precaution, undoubtedly to protect himself if things went awry.

Chernil's distance suited Tilthan just fine. He didn't care much for Chernil. The secretive employer stank of highborn snootiness. Chernil hadn't divulged much of his identity, and Tilthan didn't care to learn more. All that mattered was his ability to pay for the job he had hired them to do. And that Tilthan had verified.

"Well, boys," Tilthan said, glancing to his friends, "let's go."

With that, Tilthan maneuvered past the guardsmen. They followed a few others, finally entering the docking district.

Nath stepped ahead of Tilthan. "I think that *cheap brothel* is over there," he made a slight gesture with his forefinger. Both the phrase and gesture were a code, and in this context Nath truly meant that a dead-end alley was nearby. It would be the perfect spot to don their cloaks. After all, they didn't want to enter the city by conventional means.

2
ATOP THE CLIFFS

Now, I am well aware of how our Enemy is contained.
Nothing can break the barrier the Irum'mak'sha created.
No power in this universe can pierce that prison, except the
influence of the Au'misha'k.

Shrouded in a veil of invisibility—emitted by the
tevisral he called his thieving cloak—Tilthan scaled
the wall that divided the docking district from the
rest of Korath. His pack, too, was invisible. It seemed
whatever he held—whether in his hands, around his waist,
or over his shoulder—was also affected by the cloak.

He imagined what it might have looked like if that
weren't so. *A bag bouncing in the air*, he mused.

With catlike finesse, Tilthan eased over the wall and into
an empty alleyway. He caught sight of his friends, each
landing with the same feline grace. They too were shrouded, but Tilthan wore a pair of tevisral-spectacles that allowed him to see them.

The thieving lenses, as he called them, granted Tilthan

the ability to see various traces of magic. He primarily used them to track his fellow thieves when they too were invisible. But Tilthan could see more than that with those lenses. Much more.

Magical emissions—no matter the type—were as plain as day through those lenses. An invisibility spell? See right through it. An illusion? Easily detectable. Hidden tevisral within a wall? Not a problem. No magic could hide from him when he wore those lenses.

Tilthan caught a glance of Nemral gesturing with his hands. The thief was using a form of sign language to indicate directions. They had to go up several streets and then head east before they could reach the main road running from the docking district to the more elevated parts of the city. It was there—along the eastern cliffs—that Chernil had chosen their meeting place, an inn called the Cliffside Vista.

Once the directions to the inn were given, Nemral led them out of the alleyway.

It didn't take long for Tilthan and the others to reach the Cliffside Vista. As its name implied, the inn was on the edge of a cliff overlooking the lower parts of the city. Four stories tall, the inn was made of pale beige stone and lacked any sort of artistic architecture. One of Chernil's men stood outside, smoking a pipe.

Tilthan crept up to the bodyguard without making a noise—not even the things in his pack made the slightest sound. Tilthan stopped in front of the man, eased onto the tips of his toes, and poked the man's nose.

The bodyguard started, frantically looking about.

Tilthan stifled a growing laugh. "We're here..." he whispered slyly.

Not amused, the bodyguard turned around, heading for the inn's doors.

Out of the corner of his lenses, Tilthan caught Nath shaking his head. "I gotta have some fun, now and again," he signed, deliberately slowing his fingers to indicate a murmuring tone.

Without any further exchange, Tilthan and his thieving companions followed the bodyguard. The man deliberately left the door open longer than need be, allowing the thieves to enter.

In contrast with its plain exterior, the Cliffside Vista was quite grand on the inside. Its foyer was spacious. Lightstone chandeliers hung from the ceiling, brightly illuminating the crimson-colored room. Golden molding accented the crimson walls, forming floor-to-ceiling frames. There were a few potted plants inside, each with violet leaves—Tilthan had never seen a plant like that except in jungles.

The bodyguard nodded to a porter in the foyer, then sauntered to the dark-walnut innkeeper's desk at the back of the room.

Chernil is definitely highborn, Tilthan thought. Why else would he want to stay in a place like this? If it was up to Tilthan, they would be in some rundown place—keep the operating cost down while blending into the rabble.

The bodyguard waited at the desk for a moment, scanning the foyer. The assistant innkeeper came through an adjoining hall, asking if the bodyguard needed any help. The man just gave the assistant a cold glance, then sauntered to another hallway.

Tilthan and the others crept behind the bodyguard without drawing any attention to themselves. After all, that was their specialty.

They wound their way through several corridors, coming to a staircase that led to the upper floors. Eventually—due to the man's *slow* gait—they reached Chernil's suite.

The bodyguard opened the double doors, then stepped aside to let Tilthan and the others pass.

"We're all in," Tilthan said.

The suite's doors shut, and the bodyguard finally spoke. "You have some nerve. After that stunt you pulled I—"

"Calm down, Retarin," Chernil said, his voice coming from farther within the suite.

The bodyguard grumbled, then stalked through the suite's entrance and down a short hall leading to a common room.

"Come in, Tilthan," Chernil said. "You may sit and relax for a while. Do you care for any wine?"

"Brandleberry," Tilthan replied, unlatching his thieving cloak. He appeared from the veil of invisibility as he undid the first clasp—there was another, used to keep the cloak upon its wearer. He undid that one, too. *Whoever made the cloak was pretty smart.* The thieving cloak shimmered, glistening with white and blue light that formed a scale-like pattern. It reminded him of those mythical creatures from tales of his youth—dragons.

Nath and Nemral also appeared, carefully folding their cloaks and placing them within their packs. Tilthan, however, held onto his. *One can never be too careful,* he thought. Whenever he was on a job or adventure he liked to keep his cloak handy, on the off chance that he needed it at a moment's notice.

With his troupe all visible, Tilthan swaggered toward the common room. He still wore his thieving lenses—golden-rimmed spectacles with a bluish tint to them. Nath and Nemral, however, had put theirs away.

Inside the common room, Chernil lounged in an over-sized chair as if it were a throne. "You made good time," he said. "I take it there was no trouble breeching the walls around the docking district?"

Tilthan sighed. "Of course not. No one heard us, not even the mice."

"I didn't see any mice…" Nemral muttered.

Ignoring his friend, Tilthan continued, "So, do you have any more news about this heist?"

He suspected Chernil had somehow been receiving information while they were traveling—despite being in the middle of the ocean.

"Not yet," Chernil said. "But my contact will be arriving shortly."

"You sure have some fast messengers," Nath remarked.

"Instantaneous," Chernil said flatly.

A tevisral? Tilthan wondered. He had heard stories of being able to send messages across the world. But weren't those just *stories…?*

"That's impressive," Nemral said, nestling into a chair near Chernil.

Nath settled onto one of the couches, but Tilthan studied the common room. Floor-to-ceiling windows lined most of the exterior wall, arranged around a glass door leading to a balcony. Twilight had already settled upon Korath, and the city's lights were appearing. Tilthan could see part of the Korathi Palace from where he stood. If he were out on the balcony he probably could see all of it.

"You should take a seat, Tilthan," Chernil said firmly. "Relax a bit."

Tilthan didn't like the man's tone. He took in another sweeping glance, noting three of Chernil's bodyguards. *I wonder where the other four are?* he mused, then meandered to the couch where Nath was sitting.

"What did you think of the warning?" Nemral asked. "Did they say anything else at the border control?"

Chernil grinned. "Ghost stories," he said mockingly. "People are claiming Tefan the Headless has come to Korath, searching for his head. But we all know ghosts are not real—and if they were, they could not decapitate a man."

Another bodyguard entered the common room, carrying wineglasses and two bottles. He poured the wine as Chernil continued.

"No, they are probably dealing with a mass murderer. My guess would be a rogue mage."

"Or someone with tevisrals," Nath said.

Chernil cocked his head doubtfully. "I find that unlikely. Men with tevisrals don't tend to go on killing sprees."

"So, *every* victim has been decapitated?" Nemral asked.

Chernil shrugged. "I'm not concerned about it. The Watchmen at the border control told us of areas to avoid, and this is not one of them—neither is the palace. I—" A sudden knock sounded on the suite's door.

Tilthan strained toward the entrance, but could not hear anything else.

Retarin stalked through the common room, and the wine-bearer handed glasses to Chernil and the thieves.

"My associate, no doubt," Chernil said, sipping on his pale-blue liquor. It derived its name, keav, from its main ingredient, a blue vegetable called kealor.

Yuck... Tilthan thought. He didn't care much for keav or kealor. The vegetable was bad enough on its own— what with its bitter bite and sour aftertaste. It was even worse when distilled. How anyone could drink it was beyond him.

Footsteps echoed from the entry, and another man entered the suite's common room with Retarin. Tanned, with gray hair, the newcomer was dressed in a regal garb, a fanciful white coat covering a pale-gray doublet, both embroidered in exquisite detail. The pants were no less intricate. Chernil *had* to be highborn if he had an associate like this...

"Good evening," the newcomer said with a bow. "May the Crimson Eye remain hidden for all time!"

Chernil rose from his seat and replied the same greeting, his glass of keav still in his hand. "It is good to see you, Uligon," he smiled. "Come, sit and drink with us."

The two men took their seats, and Uligon took a glass of keav.

I can already tell I won't like him, Tilthan thought. *A man who drinks keav is a man I do not like...*

Chernil and Uligon talked in what Tilthan deemed rhetorical stuffiness. It was worse than watching a posturing match between peacocks.

Eventually, Uligon spoke of something useful. "We have two more days before the Eye of Rab'di is placed within the vault. I suggest you make your attempt during the transition."

"We don't *attempt* anything," Tilthan said sardonically, sipping on his wine. "We *accomplish*."

Uligon looked at Tilthan blankly.

"Do you know what time the transition will take place?" Chernil asked.

"After sundown," Uligon said.

"Well," Tilthan said, leaning back, "we got here with plenty of time to spare."

"I suggest you forego your ambitions for leisure and focus on your task," Uligon said with oozing contempt.

"Not a bad suggestion," Chernil chimed. "Perhaps you should go tour the palace."

Tour the palace? Tilthan was dumbfounded. The suggestion flew in the face of all his training and experience. Sure, he would scout the palace—with his tevisrals. Only an idiot would walk into the place he was about to rob. If he entered the palace, someone was bound to recognize him if things went awry.

"You obviously don't agree," Chernil said. "I'm sorry, Tilthan, but you are horrible at hiding your thoughts."

How dare he? Tilthan's temper was boiling. No one told him how to thieve. Thieving was *his* skill. He was the Master Thief, not these snooty, stuffy, highborn bastards.

"You will go to the palace," Uligon said flatly, taking another sip from his glass.

"Look," Tilthan said, rising to his feet and flashing his forefinger, "if you want this Eye-thing stolen, I'm doing it my way. We're not touring the palace. I don't *ever* want to be seen at that place." Chernil and Uligon looked at him, not amused by his outburst. "Only a fool would show himself. And furthermore, I'm not someone who you can do with as you please. I'm not your subject."

Uligon rose defiantly, and stepped toward Tilthan. "You are lucky you are useful. I have executed people for far less than your tirade."

Tilthan felt the urge to ram a dagger through Uligon's stomach, but he fought it.

"Good," Uligon said, eyeing Tilthan. "Now sit." He returned to his chair.

Tilthan, however, maneuvered around the couch, moving to the windows. He was not some pet to be ordered about.

There was more discussion about the heist, but none of that mattered to Tilthan. He would sneak into the palace and conduct his own surveilling.

———⊃•⊂———

After half an hour, Chernil watched Tilthan and his companions leave. The thief was the most irreverent man Chernil had ever met.

"We have another matter to discuss," Uligon said.

"Oh?" Chernil asked, taking another sip of his keav. He could feel its effects clouding his mind.

"These deaths are not a coincidence," Uligon said. "I *knew* some of the victims who have been murdered. They were fellow Devouts. I'm looking into the other murders to see if there are more connections."

Chernil shook his head in disbelief as Uligon continued.

"A month ago there were rumors of Tefan the Headless in Karbenath. The deaths started with a candlemaker and one of his customers. Then, the chandler's wife died, also beheaded. The death toll rose after that." Uligon groaned, taking a long swig of his keav.

"Xlyar," Chernil said, gesturing at the wine-bearer. "Another glass for my associate."

The bodyguard complied.

"Don't be stingy," Uligon urged, and Xlyar filled it to the brim. "Hundreds were dead in a matter of weeks. And no one saw anything. No witnesses. Nothing."

"What… are you getting at?" Chernil said, his voice fuzzy to his ears. "Tefan the Headless is just a ghost tale, something you frighten children with."

"You are too young," Uligon said, sighing. "This is not the first time Devouts were murdered in droves… and beheaded."

Chernil narrowed his eyes. *Is Uligon saying the folklore about Tefan is real?* But Tefan was *not* real.

"About every fifty or so years, a man is run through, then beheaded. More deaths follow, and even some disappearances." Uligon looked solemn, even frightened. "People like *us* vanish." There was a long pause before he spoke again. "I wonder if he disintegrates their corpses."

The room was starting to spin. Chernil felt the need to lie down. "I still don't see your point," he slurred.

"Someone is hunting *us*!" Uligon frowned and waved his hand in frustration. "The keav's gotten to your head. Damn keav!"

Damn good keav… Chernil grinned, feeling giddy.

"We will talk again when you are sober," Uligon said. "If I am still alive…"

3

RECONNAISSANCE

Before you patronize me, I am well aware that there is only one nicht'nal—and it can only influence the lish'sha and not any of our kind. I also know that the knowledge of creating a nicht'nal was destroyed at the end of the Thousand Years War.

Tilthan hadn't said anything since leaving Chernil's suite, and his frustrations had been building. It was only a short walk from the Cliffside Vista to the place where Chernil had reserved rooms, The Fairy and the Drake—named after a pairing in Sharzen.

As Nemral locked the door, Tilthan blurted, "You can't be serious!"

"It's what they want," Nemral retorted.

"You're *so* accommodating," Tilthan scoffed. "If they asked you to jump off a cliff, would you?" he asked sardonically.

Nath rolled his eyes. "That's hardly the same thing," the thief said. "No one is going to recognize us. When we steal the Eye of Rab'di, we will be swift and unseen."

"If nothing goes wrong," Tilthan said.

"You're sounding paranoid," Nemral muttered.

"Yeah," Nath nodded. "Looks like Iltar and Cornar are rubbing off on him."

Tilthan compressed his lips. *How dare they gang up on me?* he thought. *I'm the leader...*

"If this were Soroth or Klath I would whole-heartedly agree with you," Nath continued. "But this is Korath, practically halfway around the world from our *home*. And if what that Uligon fellow said is true, there will be so many people at the palace we will blend right in."

"You know," Tilthan said, changing the subject, "I don't trust that guy."

"Because of his choice in liquor?" Nath said. "What a poor way to judge character."

Tilthan chose not to answer.

"Well, I'm going," Nemral said. "This is probably the only time I'll get to enjoy a relaxing tour of a royal castle. Any other visit to such a place will undoubtedly involve running and hiding."

"The tour sounds like fun to me," Nath said, giving Tilthan a matter-of-fact glance.

Tilthan grunted. "Well, it's that attitude that separates the boys"—he gestured to Nath and Nemral—"from the men." He thumbed his chest.

His fellow thieves just raised their brows at him.

No matter. There was no point arguing. They had chosen the path of stupidity.

"I'm going to see if this place lives up to its name," Tilthan said and spun to the door, referring to the fortuitous pairing of drake and fairy cards in Sharzen. "Don't lock me out," he added.

"We just might," Nemral said, and Tilthan couldn't tell if he was serious or not.

The next morning, while Nath and Nemral were being idiots, Tilthan basked in his brilliance. Shrouded in his cloak, Tilthan perched atop one of the Korathi Palace's many towers—it was along the outer wall, allowing him a view to most of the palace's grounds.

The palace consisted of a cluster of domed buildings, staggered in height. Their rooftops were made of aged copper. The stone comprising the palace walls had hints of green, allowing the aged rooftops to blend into the rest of the structure. It looked to Tilthan as if some of the buildings were almost ten stories above the palace's entrance. Tilthan had seen several tall structures throughout his many adventures—though few were intact. Most buildings across Kalda rarely rose beyond five or six stories, and if they did they were probably left over from ages past.

Between the palace and the outer walls, multi-tiered gardens filled the wards packed with people.

I wonder if they think themselves safe? he mused. How much of the crowd was at the palace to see the Eye of Rab'di and how much of it was due to the murders?

People congregated in the secluded sections. Some were socializing, and others were eating. *Those definitely are seeking refuge*, he thought.

Several hours had passed when Tilthan finally tired of

his perch. He had observed the guards and their patrol routes. The palace's security was tight. Anyone attempting to scale the walls would undoubtedly be seen by a patrol or someone in the towers—unless they were invisible.

His eyes wandered beyond the palace, taking in the stunning seaside vista that stretched below the cliffs.

I suppose I should get moving.

Tilthan carefully climbed down the roof and along the tower's curved wall before gracefully landing on the ramparts.

Armored footfalls clanked behind him, and he glanced over his shoulder. Halfway between the towers, a patrol approached. He turned back to the door of the tower he had perched upon, but it was closed. Tilthan didn't dare risk opening it. He was thin enough to fit through a slightly ajar door, but then there was the possibility of a guard stationed inside the tower. He glanced over the inner parapet, eyeing a bridge that spanned the air above the gardens and connected the palace to the outer wall, one level below the ramparts. Stairs led to the bridge, between him and the patrol.

I need to get there, he thought.

Narrowing his eyes, Tilthan resolved upon a strategy. He crept toward the patrol, moving several dozen paces away from the tower's door. The farther away the better.

The patrol would be upon him in seconds. A sudden rush of exhilaration filled Tilthan. He gripped the inner parapet, then eased himself over it, hanging along the battlement. As the patrol neared, Tilthan slowed his breathing and closed his eyes. He had learned early in life that in order to sneak about, one must breathe silently. Suppressing his vision not only calmed him further, but allowed him to focus his hearing on the patrol's movements.

The patrol passed, unaware of Tilthan's presence.

Once the patrol was gone, Tilthan hefted himself back upon the ramparts and continued toward the stairs. Two guards stood as sentinels at the highest step, each holding fanisars. The staff-like weapons looked more decorative than functional. Their blades were gilded along their sides and the staffed portion held ornamental designs. The weight at the bottom of each staff was a ball with ribbed features, looking like a tiny metal pumpkin.

Soundlessly, Tilthan crept between the guards. They didn't so much as flinch at his presence. But then again, he *was* a masterful sneak.

He was on the bridge in seconds. There were no other guards around, except for those across the bridge guarding the doors to the palace. Tilthan hadn't seen a patrol cross the bridge except for once earlier that morning.

Well, now what? he wondered.

Tilthan glanced down to the gardens below the bridge. They were packed with people. The bridge was only a story and a half—maybe two—above the gardens. If the grounds had been empty he could have dropped down with ease, making only a slight sound. A few trees grew near the bridge, but attempting to climb down one would rustle the leaves. He couldn't go that way, either.

His eyes returned to the palace.

There was enough decorative stonework along the walls that he could use as handholds. The windows also had an abundance of stonework around them.

I guess that's it…

Shrugging, Tilthan crossed the bridge. Once he was a dozen paces away from the guards at the doors, he eased himself over the bridge's parapet and shimmied toward the palace's outer wall. He was down in the gardens soon after, carefully moving around shrubbery.

There was enough noise from the crowd that he could move without being heard.

Tilthan moved through the throng, easing through gaps. It was so easy. One of his earliest training exercises after receiving his thieving cloak was to navigate Klath's Central Highway while invisible. It was the busiest street in the city. The roads from each of the city's gates emptied into the Central Highway, as well as dozens of other streets. The entire highway was like one enormous market, always full of people, even at night. The Central Highway was tricky enough to navigate when visible, but becoming invisible made it much more difficult. Not to mention the consequences of being caught wearing a magical cloak...

All in all, the Central Highway was a formidable proving ground.

After a while, Tilthan was on the path leading to the palace's main gate. It was a hustle and bustle of people going to and fro. Children played, running back and forth. A crier announced an upcoming tour of the palace. A curator passed by, proclaiming the various items on display. Chatter from people in the gardens filled the air. Even if he hadn't been wearing his cloak, Tilthan could have blended into the crowd.

Tilthan returned his attention to the crier. "...in the northern courtyard. Come see the Eye of Rab'di, the fabled jewel that once sat above the throne of Emperor

Karath the First. Tours run every half an hour. Gather your party and join us in the northern courtyard…"

Northern courtyard, huh?

That gave Tilthan a wicked idea, wickedly awesome. He would go on that tour—just not how Chernil had suggested.

Swiftly, Tilthan wove through the busy throng. The playing children proved a fun challenge, as they were totally unpredictable—but not even they touched him. He came to a branching path leading to the northern wards, but it was jam-packed. Instead of waiting for an opening, Tilthan leapt onto a knee-high wall hemming the garden's plants from the path. He danced his way past the dense crowd, then hurried to the northern courtyard.

Another tour must have just run because the courtyard was mostly empty. The sparse crowd was pressed along the edges of the courtyard, gathered beneath the trees in the warmth of the late fall weather.

Tilthan meandered into the center of the courtyard, feeling an irresistible urge to dance. He often felt like that after a victory, and navigating the busy wards of the palace was a victory. Sort of.

A beat formed in Tilthan's head, resembling one of his favorite songs. It was as if it were *actually* playing within the courtyard.

Suddenly, he broke into a dance, soundlessly moving across the stone ground.

People trickled into the courtyard, and Tilthan kept dancing. He imagined what it would have been like if he were visible. There would be applause and cheering. His dancing would be infectious. It always was. Others would gather around him, mimicking his dance-moves. Occasionally, a pretty face would show, and that often led to something else entirely.

Tilthan loved dancing.

Amid a spin, Tilthan caught sight of Nath. His fellow thief stood near the entrance of the courtyard, shrouded in his cloak and wearing his thieving lenses.

"What do you think you're doing?" Nath signed.

Still dancing, Tilthan signed his reply. "Killing time. Ya know."

Nath rolled his eyes. A moment later, Nemral entered the courtyard, also concealed.

"Why don't you join me?" Tilthan signed, spinning once again.

"I don't dance," Nemral signed, his movements exaggerated and deliberate. He was not amused.

"Well, if you want to be a masterful thief you need to know how to dance," Tilthan signed. "It's all about footwork."

More people filed into the courtyard, and Tilthan continued dancing. He caught sight of an attractive woman in a dark green dress with fine embroidery. Her dark-brown-almost-black hair curled past her shoulders to lie against her breasts. If Tilthan had been visible he would have approached her.

The beautiful woman came toward him, eyeing everyone in the courtyard. "We will begin the next tour shortly," the woman said. "My name is Cilara, and I will be your guide today. Please gather around me."

Guess I'm done, Tilthan thought, finishing with a flashy movement. He then hurried toward his invisible companions.

"How long is the tour?" Tilthan signed.

"A little over an hour," Nath replied, his fingers moving swiftly.

Soon, they were inside the palace. Not only was this a tour of the various artistic pieces, it was also a thorough walkthrough of the Korathi Palace's common rooms. Cilara was very detailed in her explanations.

Brains and beauty, Tilthan thought, amused and intrigued. He *could* like that woman.

Though there were art pieces in the palace's grand foyer and in other halls, the main exhibit was in the audience chamber at the palace's heart.

The chamber was a rectangular room three stories tall. Tilthan hadn't visited many audience chambers, but this one was bigger than a ship. Balconies lined the highest floor on three sides, held up by two-story pillars. Aged copper trusses lined the ceiling, creating nine large rectangles. Nine elaborate chandeliers hung from the ceiling, housing glistening gems and vibrant lightstones.

Armored guards stood at each of the entrances—the main double doors and two one-story corridors positioned halfway through the audience chamber. Tilthan counted at least twelve guards, not to mention those inside.

The Korathi nobles weren't taking any chances.

Six rows of display cases and elegant easels lined much of the audience chamber. All six rows flowed to the back of the room.

"The Eye is up there," Nath signed to Tilthan.

Nemral gestured for Tilthan to follow, and the three of them skipped ahead of the tour. They went straight for the back, toward a dais beneath floor-to-ceiling windows lining the far wall. Each window was divided into nine rectangles like the trusses on the ceiling.

At the foot of the dais, the Eye of Rab'di—a large red sphere about twice the size of a man's head—was encased within a squared glass display case atop a gaudy pedestal. The oversized gem was semi-translucent, with swirling patterns of oranges and yellows that shifted ever so slightly. There was a vibrant hue around the Eye, denoting magical emissions.

Tilthan adjusted his spectacles, looking at the Eye of Rab'di without the magical lenses. The oversized gem didn't glow, nor were the swirling patterns present.

It's a tevisral, he marveled. Chernil had left that part out—but perhaps he didn't know. Tilthan pushed aside the notion as he remembered that strange greeting Chernil and Uligon exchanged. It mentioned a Crimson Eye. *Is this that Crimson Eye?* he wondered. The Eye of Rab'di *was* red, and it *was* round. Those swirling patterns *did* look like a iris… and, it was literally called an eye.

Tilthan thought on the greeting further. The phrasing implied they were vowing to keep the Crimson Eye hidden. Is that why they wanted Tilthan to steal the Eye of Rab'di? So they could hide it again? It seemed such a waste to throw away something like *this*.

Despite spending two months with Chernil, Tilthan had never asked *why* he wanted them to steal the Eye of Rab'di. The speculations sent Tilthan's mind spinning.

Attempting to wash away the confusion, Tilthan read-
justed his spectacles and searched the display case. Because of the glow surrounding the Eye of Rab'di, he
couldn't tell if there were any traps using magic. But there
was no trace of magic within the pedestal. He thought he
saw a seam between the display case and the pedestal, but
he couldn't be sure without closer inspection. He *might* be
able to get that close.

Tilthan edged toward the red rope between him and the
case, but he still couldn't get close enough. If the display
case was trapped he wouldn't be able to know for certain
until they enacted the deed.

Four guards stood at each corner of the Eye's display,
completely motionless. They were dressed in thick plate
armor. Two wielded great-swords and two wielded
fanisars. There were eight other guards in the room.

Twelve, huh? They could steal the Eye now and it
wouldn't prove too much of a challenge. They could kill
three instantly. The others would go down quick, as long
as no mages came. A mage could briefly disrupt his cloak's
veil of invisibility with a dispel, although the concealing
magic would resume immediately after the dispel dissipated.

Nevertheless, it would still prove more favorable to steal
the gem during its return to the vault. Chernil's friend,
Uligon, claimed the Eye's escorts would decrease to six
guards at a certain corridor.

A tap on Tilthan's shoulder drew his attention.

"Our guide mentioned the vault is that way," Nath
signed, then pointed to the corridor to their left.

"Let's go check it out then," Tilthan suggested, swaggering away from the well-guarded display. He was still in a good mood, and he danced with each step.

4

FOLKTALES

*Logically, this should be enough to ease any concern. But the
followers of our Enemy believe otherwise. And that belief
stirs my worry.*

After scouting the way to the vault, Tilthan and the
others returned to The Fairy and the Drake.

It was near dinner time, and Tilthan groaned,
rubbing his empty belly. "I'm famished," he said.

"There was a food cart outside the palace gates,"
Nemral said. "You could have eaten instead of being so
insistent on remaining hidden."

Tilthan gave Nemral a sullen look.

Once they returned their thieving tevisrals to their
room, Tilthan and the others ventured into the dining hall
of the inn. Tilthan stepped ahead of his fellow thieves,
hands on hips as he surveyed the tavern.

The inn was of considerable size, so it made sense that
its tavern would accommodate a couple hundred patrons.
There were tables scattered throughout the space and

booths along the walls. A large L-shaped bar took up one side of the room, with seats for over twenty. There was even a stage where a small group of musicians were setting up their instruments.

"Not bad," Tilthan said with a nod. "Not bad at all."

Nemral pushed past Tilthan and moved for one of the empty booths. Nath followed him, but Tilthan remained at the entrance.

Near the stage, several workers were clearing away some empty tables. *Making room for a dance floor, maybe?*

He smiled and joined his friends at the booth, and dinner appeared soon after. It consisted of a well-plated meal of crotu—a yellow-fleshed fish native to the Sea of Korath—seared vegetables, and soft flatbread.

It was a good thing they had arrived when they did, as the tavern began to fill with patrons. The musicians had finished their preparations and now started playing a lively tune.

As the thieves finished eating, Tilthan noticed a group of women entering the tavern. He quickly evaluated each of them. One looked a tad overdressed, and her makeup was a bit garish. Another was less showy, but not unattractive. There was a set of twins, both tall, well-tanned, and haughty. And then—

Oh my... Tilthan's lips curled into a grin, as his eyes fell upon a familiar face.

It was the tour guide, Cilara.

Her dark-brown-almost-black hair was pulled back into curly a ponytail, and a bit of makeup brightened her face. Her eyes, though... Had they been *that* blue? She was by far the most attractive woman he had encountered on this trip to Korath.

Cilara moved through the tavern with the other women, who took seats at the bar near the stage.

"You boys want some drinks?" Tilthan asked his fellow thieves, but his eyes were on Cilara.

"You buyin'?" Nath asked. Tilthan shot Nath a perturbed glance.

"I'll take some brandy," Nemral said. "Whatever kind they have."

Nodding, Tilthan slid out of the booth. "Speak now or—"

"Just some ale," Nath said. "I don't want to be too intoxicated."

Tilthan swaggered across the tavern, weaving around the patrons filing toward the stage. He moved toward Cilara and one of the twins. Several men were already engaging the twins in small talk. Neither seemed interested.

Cilara, however, quietly stared toward the stage, listening to the music.

Perfect, Tilthan thought, maneuvering directly into her field of vision. He ignored her initially, searching for the bartender.

"What brandy do you carry?" Tilthan hollered to the bartender.

"Colvin and Fedirm."

"Give me one of each," Tilthan said, "and the lightest ale you've got. My friend can't hold his liquor." Cilara snickered from beside Tilthan, and he shot her an aloof glance. She simply grinned at him.

"What...?" he asked innocently. "He *really* can't hold it. You should see what happens when he takes a sip of brandleberry—Oh! You're that tour guide, from the palace." He squinted and playfully waggled his finger. "Aren't you?"

"I am," Cilara said, looking surprised.

"You must not recognize me," Tilthan said. "It's okay. I can't expect you to remember *every* handsome face."

Cilara chuckled, a smile forming upon her lips.

"You know your stuff, though," Tilthan turned back toward the bar, briefly searching for the bartender before returning his gaze to Cilara. "Your descriptions of Moskian art were quite thorough."

"Thank you," she said, her smile broadening.

Tilthan focused on her eyes, studying her pupils. *They are dilating.*

"I take it you were educated as a historian," he added. "But you must not have studied here."

"In Kildath," she said.

The bartender returned with a stein of ale. "Do you want that brandy warmed?"

"Sure," Tilthan said, taking the stein. "I'll be back." He swaggered away from the bar, moving in a wide arc that kept him in Cilara's field of view. Arriving back at their table, he slid the stein to Nath.

"Who is that woman you're talking to?" Nath asked.

"Don't recognize her?" Tilthan grinned, then returned to the bar. The warmed brandy was already waiting for him.

With the glasses in hand, Tilthan searched for the bartender. He was busy with another patron.

"You wouldn't mind doing me a favor, would you?" he asked Cilara.

She nodded.

"Could you order some messel for me?"

"Let me guess," she grinned. "That's for your other friend?"

Tilthan feigned an appalled expression. "Why, no! It's for me." He turned around, moving back toward Nath and Nemral. The messel he had requested was a hot drink made from the sweet inner bark of a tree sharing the same name. Messel was often used as a stimulant.

As Tilthan approached his friends, Nath looked at him, demanding an answer. "That's the tour guide!" he said through clenched teeth.

"What happened to your 'I don't want to be seen' bit?" Nemral asked.

Tilthan lowered his eyebrows in annoyance, and set the glasses of brandy on the table.

"You're a hypocrite, you know that?" Nath said.

"I'm not a hypocrite," Tilthan said. "She never actually *saw* me at the palace. That's a big difference."

Nath was about to roll his eyes but Tilthan spun around, avoiding the disdainful gesture. He was soon back at the bar with Cilara.

"I placed your order," she said.

Tilthan smiled. "I appreciate that. I just got to have my messel." He didn't actually require the drink. Asking for it was one of those ploys he used to showcase his self-confidence. Ordering hot messel during a warm time of year was quirky. And Tilthan *owned* that quirk.

They continued talking about particular pieces of art Tilthan had observed during the tour. He wasn't an art connoisseur by any means, but he did know a little bit

about things that would find their home in a museum—
after all, Tilthan had accompanied Iltar and Cornar on
many an adventure that discovered such things. Those two
had a knack for turning a piece of garbage into something
museum-worthy.

After a while, they began talking about the Eye of
Rab'di.

"Have you heard that the Eye of Rab'di is *actually* a
tevisral?" Tilthan asked.

Cilara laughed, spitting part of her ale into her stein.
"You're joking," she said amid her mirth.

Tilthan shook his head. "Nah, I'm dead serious. I don't
remember all the details, but I heard it had magical proper-
ties to it."

She didn't look convinced.

"I heard another rumor about it, too," he said, leaning
closer to Cilara. "A long time ago, a group of people
wanted to keep the Eye of Rab'di hidden. They made a
pact so it would never come to light. They called it, "The
Crimson Eye," or so I heard…"

Cilara looked like she was about to laugh again. "Do
these people have a name for themselves?" she asked.

"Not that I know of," Tilthan shrugged, then leaned
back. He had to come up with more of this fictional tale,
but nothing was coming to mind. "They say those people
are ever watchful for when the Crimson Eye resurfaces."
He left it at that.

Cilara was thoroughly entertained. "I'll have to tell my
friend all this," she gestured to the woman who had too
much makeup on. "Her brother, Jaedrin, was on the expe-
dition that found the Eye of Rab'di."

"Oh?"

"Jaedrin is actually the one who unearthed it," Cilara said. "Sire Duarin was receiving supplies from some tribesmen they had come across earlier in their trip. They go by some weird name"—she waved her hand—"Yelin-something. I don't remember their name, exactly. But they live in a place called the High Valley." She leaned close and lowered her voice. "I *hear* they make scarecrows of people if they wander into places they shouldn't." Cilara paused, then took a swig of her ale. "Now, that's something I didn't include on the tour."

Tilthan grinned. *I could have plenty of fun with this woman...*

Their conversation continued well into the night. At one point, Tilthan rested his hand beside Cilara's drink, and eventually she teased him with her touch.

From there, Tilthan escalated his means of seduction. He played off her cues, knowing when and how to increase the sexual tension between them. Not only was he a master thief, but an expert philanderer, too. They were soon dancing together. Cilara seemed to be enjoying herself, and so was Tilthan.

As they danced, Tilthan noticed Nath gesturing for him to come near.

"Will you excuse me for a moment?" he asked, waiting for her approval. She studied him briefly, then nodded. "I'll be right back," he said with a grin, then hurried toward his thieving companions.

"We're going to go to the palace," Nath whispered. "I want to see how they run their patrols at night."

"Don't get caught," Tilthan said with a chuckle. "Or beheaded. You aren't me, after all."

Nath rolled his eyes. "Don't have *too* much fun."

"You know me," Tilthan said, and grinned.

"Yeah, I do," Nath said. "One of these days I'd like to know how many children you have scattered across Kalda."

Tilthan shook his head, then returned to Cilara. There was a yearning in her eyes.

"Do you want to get out of here?" he asked.

She nodded. "I live nearby. We could go there."

Tilthan liked the sound of that. Eager for the *best* kind of nightly fun, he took her hand and guided her out of the tavern.

———◁•▷———

It was late when Tilthan returned to his room at The Fairy and the Drake. Nath and Nemral sat on their beds, looking frightened. They both wore their spectacles and cloaks, though the latter were not activated.

"What's wrong with you two?" Tilthan asked sardonically.

Nath looked at Tilthan with wide eyes, but Nemral was the first to speak.

"It seems Tefan *really* is here," Nemral said, sounding frazzled. He nervously adjusted his spectacles.

Tilthan burst into laughter. "You... you *actually* believe that nonsense? Come on, Nemral."

Nath folded his arms, and he gave Tilthan a look that said, "You really should listen."

Not you, too, Tilthan thought, furrowing his brow. He pursed his lips and studied Nemral.

"Nem, remember what we used to do as kids?" Tilthan asked. "The *hoaxes* we played on the farmers out in the northern fields and across the river?" Nemral gave him a sullen look. "We fooled them into thinking vampires were after their piggies, their sweet, sweet piggies. But vampires aren't real! And now, here in Korath, someone is doing just that—but to people." It was a tad cruel. Who knew, maybe those people deserved to die. "Whoever is responsible for the killings is probably going out of their way to add a dramatic flair to their crime. They are creating a mystique to bedazzle their next victim."

Sighing, Nemral looked to Nath, who said nothing.

"What?" Tilthan demanded.

"If you stop blabbering I'll tell you," Nemral said.

Taken aback, Tilthan started. Nemral had grown a backbone over the years. *I guess adulthood does that...*

"We *saw* him, Tilthan," Nemral insisted. "We saw him!"

"You're sure?" Tilthan said, skepticism filling his voice.

Nath nodded.

"It was after we investigated the palace," Nemral said. "We returned here to secure our *things*, then went out for a drink—the tavern here was closed. We weren't too far away when I thought I heard a muffled sound down an alleyway. I motioned to Nath, and we crept toward a dead-end. We found a big burly man holding a shimmering sword. A smaller man was entangled in some kind of vine, and they were just staring at each other. Then, the big man decapitated his victim.

"Nath backed up immediately, and I peeled away. It was scary, Tilthan. Scary! When I went to peer back around the corner, the man with the sword was gone. All that was left was a headless corpse."

"And we didn't hear an incantation either," Nath interjected. "Nor did he have a cloak like ours."

"It *was* Tefan," Nemral said, shaking his head. He then recounted the whimsical tale, a folktale Tilthan had heard several times as a child.

Tefan the Headless, executed for his furious crimes of passion, roamed the world in search of his head. It was said that in life Tefan was a cruel man, butchering men, women, and children. He slew whole families. Some iterations were more gruesome than others, details no child should ever hear.

The sites of Tefan's massacres varied. Some claimed small towns and villages in the Western Sovereignty as the place of the violent butchery. Others cited remote parts of the Kingdom of Los, particularly in what were now Gastrim and Kerindor. One particular retelling even claimed the early city of Rystra as the place of Tefan's bloodbath. But no one knew for sure.

Ultimately, Tefan was caught, tried, and executed by beheading. But before his execution, an old woman came to Tefan, pronouncing a curse upon him. Tefan's soul would never know peace. He would writhe in agony for all eternity. When he was dead, the old woman took his head and burned it. That act initiated Tefan's eternal punishment, and so his soul wandered the world in search of his head.

The tale was rather ridiculous, especially when one understood the laws of magic. Tilthan didn't claim to be an absolute authority on the subject—he was no mage. But what the folktale of Tefan claimed possible was pure fantasy. It was impossible.

"There's got to be another explanation," Tilthan chuckled nervously. "I mean, was this fellow headless? After all, in the tale, Tefan is dead."

Nemral shook his head. "This has happened before. Fifty years ago, in Voglin."

Voglin? *Where was that?*

"Fifty years before that, in a small town outside of Estrom, in Kaladorn," Nemral continued, "the same thing happened that is happening here in Korath."

The thief's expression was solemn.

Well, Nemral will get along with Hagen, Tilthan thought. The short illusionist was fond of telling ghost stories, and it seemed Hagen believed every single one of them.

"We need to be careful," Nemral insisted warily. "I heard that if you witness Tefan taking a head, he'll come for yours."

"That's news to me…" Nath said, sounding skeptical.

Nemral, however, wrapped his thieving cloak about him, latched the clasp to activate the tevisral, and disappeared. "I'm sleeping invisibly," he said in a shaky voice.

Tilthan turned to Nath, but the other thief was silent. He looked traumatized. Tilthan and Nath had been through quite a bit, what with the adventures with Iltar and Cornar. Never before had Tilthan seen Nath so spooked.

Perhaps ghosts are real, he thought. If they were, there was nothing Tilthan could do about it. Shrugging off the matter, Tilthan climbed into bed. He needed to sleep.

Tomorrow was going to be a big day.

5

AN ILLICIT VISIT

A prophecy contained within our Enemy's accursed scriptures claims, "The Crimson Eye will shine white, and its power will shackle its creators." The passage further explains that this change will occur during the awakening of the Unspoken One.

A storm moved in from the east, dousing Korath in a violent downpour. The storm lasted most of the day, ruining Tilthan's plans. He had intended to sneak into the palace grounds during the day, lying in wait until the gates were closed. But, despite their cloaks, the rain would give them away. A few sprinkles wouldn't matter, but a downpour such as the one assailing the city would reveal their invisible outlines. People would probably mistake *them* for Tefan the Headless.

The storm eventually let up around sunset.

Tilthan and the others swiftly departed The Fairy and the Drake. Wary of being seen, Tilthan led his fellow thieves through alleys and side streets toward the palace.

They neared the main road leading to the palace gates at twilight.

Tilthan emerged from an alleyway only to find the palace gates closing. *Damn*, he cursed to himself, then glimpsed movement from Nemral's fingers.

"What do we do now?" the thief signed.

"Scale the walls," Nath signed, his fingers moving matter-of-factly.

There was no other way.

Pursing his invisible lips, Tilthan scanned the walls. "Let's go to our egress point," he signed. "We can try to get in that way."

The place Tilthan had chosen was to the west of the palace walls, near an aqueduct that ran beside the Korathi Palace. The aqueduct emptied into a man-made reservoir that then sent water to the lower parts of the city near the docking district. The reservoir was about three stories tall, maybe even closer to four. But the palace walls were still a story higher, not to mention that the distance between the thieves and the reservoir was greater than five stories.

"The sooner we get done with this, the better," Nemral signed.

"Scared, Nem?" Tilthan signed, grinning. His tone would have been mocking if he were speaking.

Nemral didn't reply.

"Are you thinking we swing from the top of the reservoir?" Nath signed. "It's not tall enough."

Tilthan nodded. "We can use the momentum to get us close enough to throw another rope onto the outer battlement," he signed.

"That sounds convoluted," Nemral signed slowly. He

wasn't amused.

"Then we tie the ropes together," Tilthan suggested. He used his hands to illustrate the maneuver. The second rope would have a climbing hook on one end to catch the battlement between the crenels. It made perfect sense to him.

They scaled the aqueduct and secured the rope to the inner railing along the reservoir's ramparts. Since the thieves were touching the rope, it was invisible, and remained that way even after they secured it to the railing.

Tilthan grabbed the end of the rope, tying another to it. "Here I go," he whispered, tossing part of the rope over the wall. He gave the rope some slack then hurried along the ramparts and toward the aqueduct leading to the lower parts of the city. Tilthan was almost to the aqueduct when he came to the knot between the ropes.

Perfect, he thought. Tilthan studied the distance and the angle between him and the palace walls. It would be a tricky throw.

The thrill of the theft swelled inside him, and Tilthan burst into a dash, leaping over the reservoir wall. He swung through the air, nearing the ground, but he threw his feet forward and swung upward. He caught a glimpse of his companions, then felt his ascent slowing.

Now!

He threw the second rope, watching the climbing hook sail through the air. The rope reached the palace's battlement as he became weightless—the sensation, however, didn't last long.

Still clutching the rope, Tilthan began falling backward, but abruptly stopped as the climbing hook caught the battlement with a faint ting. He jolted backward and swung like a pendulum. Tilthan threw his feet out, catching the rope. His momentum, however, carried through the rope, causing him to swing.

Easy, he thought, *too easy*.

Once the rope stilled, Tilthan climbed it to the palace walls. He was two thirds of the way to the ramparts when a patrol marched by. They passed by his invisible climbing hook, completely unaware.

Tilthan made it onto the ramparts just as the patrol disappeared into one of the towers. *Well, that was perfect timing*, he thought. Another patrol wouldn't be by for at least a quarter of an hour.

Holding the rope, Tilthan watched as Nath untied the end attached to the reservoir's railing. The rope swung toward the palace walls, draping along the street, where Nemral swiftly coiled it.

It wasn't long before the other thieves joined Tilthan on the ramparts. As they gathered, droplets began pelting them.

"Now where?" Nemral signed. "How are we going to get inside?"

"Don't worry," Nath signed. "I saw some servant quarters along the more secluded parts of the wards. We can sneak in through one of the windows."

"You've always had a thing for serving wenches..." Tilthan signed with sarcasm, implying that Nath had obtained the information while peeping on the palace's female staff.

Nath shook his head, his expression serious. "Someone has to come up with a backup when your plan fails. I doubt the servant quarters will be guarded."

Tilthan pursed his lips, watching as Nath pointed to a nearby bridge. It was similar to the one Tilthan had traversed the day before.

The three of them moved as one, stopping partway across the bridge. Tilthan glanced to where the bridge and palace met. Two guards stood at attention beside double doors. Stifling a sigh, Tilthan slid his hand along the railing, but the stone was too slick to climb safely.

There was only one alternative. He hoped it wouldn't be too loud.

"Let's drop down," Tilthan signed, but Nath was already over the railing.

One by one, the thieves landed in the courtyard. They splashed in puddles, but the splashing didn't draw the attention of the guards above.

Tilthan looked to the bridge, grinning triumphantly.

"This way," Nath signed.

The thieves hurried through the courtyard, making their way to a more secluded part of the palace's wards. They climbed a short flight of steps, and Nath moved into the shrubbery along the palace wall. The thief stopped beneath a window half a story above them.

"You couldn't have picked something ground level?" Tilthan signed.

Nath gave Tilthan an unamused glance, then tested the decorative stonework on the wall. Though it was wet, Nath was able to make the climb to the window.

While Nath examined the window, Tilthan looked about the courtyard. All was silent, except for faint splashing footfalls on the palace's outer walls. Tilthan expected more security at the palace. *Perhaps the bulk of their guards are in-*

side? he thought.

A creaking hinge carried through the air, and Tilthan spun. Nath was climbing through the window, and Nemral was partway up the wall. Tilthan quickly followed them, and all three thieves were inside within seconds. They stood in a plain-looking sitting room with worn furniture. There were no other windows besides the one they had entered, but there were several doors along each wall.

As Tilthan went to close the window, one of the doors opened. He froze, hand still gripping the open pane.

A feminine sigh filled the room, followed by a grumbling complaint. A short woman in a bathrobe stomped from the open door, shaking her head. "I thought they fixed that," she groused, approaching Tilthan.

Cautiously, Tilthan backed up, letting the pane sway on its hinges. He moved silently across a rug, easing toward his fellow thieves.

The woman grumbled again as she shut the window, then moved toward a different doorway, revealing a steamy bath. She disrobed as she entered, and then quickly shut the door behind her.

Tilthan caught his two friends' eyes lingering on the now-shut door.

"The show is over," Tilthan signed, then moved toward a door across from the window. "You can peep later."

The door was locked, and Tilthan pressed his ear to the door. There was no sound beyond it.

Ever careful, Tilthan unlocked the door and cracked it ajar. Again, there was no sound. Satisfied, he moved through the doorway, finding himself in one of the palace's many corridors. Nath and Nemral joined him soon after.

The two thieves kept their eyes on either end of the corridor as Tilthan re-secured the door. Then he removed a thin rod twice the length of a finger—another of his thieving tevisrals. The rod could be used to disarm mechanical mechanisms and disrupt coursing magic within tevisrals. Tilthan had used it many a time.

He swiftly maneuvered the rod toward the lock, and it shifted to conform to the shape of the keyhole. A faint click echoed from the lock. Satisfied, Tilthan gestured for the others to continue down the hall.

———————◆•◆———————

The thieves meandered through the western parts of the palace, moving from building to building. As they rounded one of the outer halls of the palace's main keep, a faint conversation filtered into the corridor.

"…is getting out of control, I tell you," a man said. "Someone has to stop this madman."

The conversation grew louder, accompanied by clinking armor. Tilthan motioned for his thieving companions to press themselves against the wall.

"I can't believe it," a second voice said with a sigh. "Twenty-seven more found today… twenty-seven!"

Nemral glanced to Tilthan. "A patrol?" the thief signed.

Tilthan shrugged.

"There has to be more than one murderer," a third voice said.

At that moment, a patrol of six guards—each clad in plated armor and wielding fanisars—entered the hall, marching toward Tilthan and the others.

"No one man could kill that many people and remain hidden," the third voice continued, coming from the lead guard. "It has to be a renegade cabal."

"A lone mage would be capable of such destruction," the guard beside the leader interjected flatly.

"The only mages skilled enough to pull off such a massacre are Losians," the first voice said, coming from the back. "And I *doubt* a Losian is behind this bloodbath."

"Why not?" a man from the middle asked. "They attacked Mindolarn."

"It's the ghost of Tefan," a different guard replied. "He *is* the only explanation."

The lead guard shook his head, passing Tilthan and the others. "A ghost?" He snorted in derision. "How can you attribute three hundred deaths to a ghost?"

The guard who mentioned Tefan frowned, but didn't say anymore. Each of the guards in the patrol continued voicing their speculation, then disappeared down the hall.

"Three hundred dead?" Nath signed, looking to Tilthan and Nemral with wide eyes.

"The sooner we finish this the better," Nemral signed, hurrying down the hall.

Tilthan drew his lips tight, trying not to show his amusement for the topic of Tefan the Headless. He watched his friends turn a corner as the hall became quiet—only the faint pitter-patter of rain against the windows broke the silence.

He took one step forward, but an odd flash of movement beyond the window caught his eye. Tilthan spun just as a masculine figure *leapt over* the palace's outer wall.

Tilthan started, his eyes wide. *Impossible!* His eyes focused on the man now rebounding through the palace wards. The stranger was shrouded in invisibility magic and glowed with a white aura—the sign of an enhancing spell. It wasn't long before the stranger vanished.

That must have been how he cleared the wall. But never had Tilthan seen someone *leap* five stories. That was beyond any mage's skill—at least he assumed.

A knot formed in Tilthan's stomach, and he hurried after Nath and Nemral. He was almost running. As he caught up to his compatriots, Tilthan drew their attention. "I just saw *something*," he signed. "Something impossible." Nath and Nemral looked surprised.

"A man *leapt* over the palace walls," Tilthan signed.

Nemral paled. "Wh-what did he look like?" The thief's fingers stumbled through his signing.

"I didn't get a good look," Tilthan replied, his fingers moving swiftly. "But I think we have some competition."

———◦•◦———

The three thieves soon arrived at the audience chamber, but it was well guarded. The main doors were shut, and the corridors leading to the side entrances were blocked by barricades and guardsmen.

Tilthan guided the others up to the audience chamber's third floor, but the entrances to the balconies were also guarded.

Tilthan signed a vulgar curse.

"There are only two at each door," Nemral signed.

Nath shook his head. "These halls will undoubtedly

have patrols," he signed. "We can't risk it."

"Is there anything above the chamber?" Nemral signed. "Maybe we can drop in from above the trusses?"

Tilthan peeled away silently, hurrying down the hall. He glanced over his shoulder, watching as the other thieves followed him. Was there a maintenance access somewhere? Tilthan searched the halls branching off from those around the audience chamber. Eventually, he came to a narrow dead-end hallway with a single unguarded door.

Intrigued, Tilthan crept to the door and tried its handle. It was locked, but he managed to open it with his thieving rod. Beyond the door was a narrow flight of stairs leading up into darkness. Its appearance was less refined than the rest of the palace.

"Are you sure this will lead to the audience chamber?" Nath signed.

"It's worth looking into," Tilthan signed with agitation, then hurried up the stairs.

Though the space beyond the steps was dark, Tilthan's spectacles adjusted to the lack of light. He could see the vast attic as if it were lit by dozens of lightstones. Stone-and-wood pillars held up slanting ceilings, and crude planks of wood sprawled across the floor.

Tilthan carefully retraced his steps, moving to what he hoped was the ceiling of the audience chamber. Both Nath and Nemral fanned out, searching the floor.

"I think I found it," Nath whispered.

Tilthan spun. Nath stood above a hidden door among the crude planks. "Why don't you take a look?" Tilthan asked.

Though his gaze was focused on the door in the floor, Nath rolled his eyes. He lifted the door enough for him to peek through, but soon shut it. "That's it all right, but the guards are getting ready to move the Eye."

Tilthan hurried to the door, lifting it gently. The balcony overlooking the audience chamber was directly beneath the hidden door. Clinking armor and heavy footfalls echoed into the attic. "Down we go!" Tilthan whispered, further opening the door. He eased through the opening, landing soundlessly. Not that it mattered. There was enough noise in the audience chamber to muffle his landing.

He hurried away, allowing Nath and Nemral to descend.

As the others landed on the balcony, Tilthan surveyed the audience chamber. The exhibits—all but the display case containing the Eye of Rab'di—were cleared from the floor, and thirty guards shuffled through the room. A familiar voice sounded amid the clinking armor, giving orders.

No... Tilthan's eyes widened, settling upon the source of the familiar voice. A tanned old man with gray hair, dressed in a regal garb, crossed the room, weaving past the guards. *That bastard...* That old man was none other than Chernil's associate, Uligon.

6

THE DEED

Many of the defiled believe that the Unspoken One's advent is at hand. I also believe it. I have probed the minds of many—far too many—and I am as convinced as they are.

Tilthan should have figured Uligon was closely involved with the Eye of Rab'di. How else would the man have known the details about the gem's transfer?

"Is that who I think it is?" Nemral signed.

Nath nodded.

Uligon joined another regal-looking fellow. This second man looked younger than Uligon, but had a superior demeanor about him.

"...I have doubled the guard escort," Uligon said, his voice echoing through the audience chamber. "What with the recent murders we cannot be too cautious, Sire Duarin."

So, that's the man who found it, Tilthan mused.

Guards parted for the two men as Uligon and Duarin

proceeded to the display case holding the Eye of Rab'di.

"So, does that mean there will be twelve instead of six?" Nemral signed, referring to what Uligon had told them. They knew thirty guards were escorting the Eye from the audience chamber, but that would dwindle to six.

"It doesn't matter," Tilthan signed. "Even if there are twelve we can dispatch them quick."

"...I appreciate your concern," Sire Duarin said, his voice deep and rich. "But I doubt an incident will occur tonight. The City Watch has devised a theory to this madness, and that theory proves the palace safe."

Uligon didn't look convinced.

The two men stopped at the display case, inspecting it. Guards filled in around them, creating a partial ring that wrapped partway up the dais. They were all focused on the Eye of Rab'di, ignoring the storm brewing beyond the towering windows.

A flash of lightning lit the audience chamber as Tilthan began to sign to his fellow thieves. He stopped abruptly, focusing on a masculine figure darkening a spot on the upper panes of the floor-to-ceiling windows. With curiosity, Tilthan leaned forward, bracing himself against the balcony's railing. His eyes widened as the burly man *climbed* down the upper panes of the far window, glowing with a white aura. The man's hands seemed to stick to the glass.

You again... Tilthan murmured. It seemed someone else wanted the Eye of Rab'di.

"By Dorin's Scepter!" Nemral swore under his breath. "Th-tha-that's...."

"How... is he climbing?" Nath muttered.

The burly man stopped short of the middle panes, placing one hand upon the glass below his waist. The man's hand glowed with pale brown-gray light that soon shot through the rest of the pane. Tilthan could see a ripple move through the glass, changing it. None of the men in the audience chamber seemed to notice. *Is he transmuting—?*

Suddenly, the burly man swung *through* the window, gracefully falling onto the dais without shattering the pane. His veil of invisibility dissipated as he rose to his feet, and he stretched out his hand. Within a heartbeat, a shaft of shimmering green light formed—a sword composed of pure magic.

"That's Tefan!" Nemral croaked.

Tilthan started. Was this *really* the ghost of a dead man? *No*, Tilthan told himself, *he's using magic. He has to be a mage, a renegade mage.* But Tilthan had never seen a mage muster magic as swiftly as this man.

"That's him," Nath whispered through clenched teeth. "The one from the alley. The murderer!"

At that moment, Uligon and the others noticed the newcomer. A cacophony of singing metal, clinking armor, and frantic shouts filled the audience chamber. Amid the noises several men cried, "Sound the alarm!" Guards spun, dropping into battle stances.

Great... Tilthan sighed.

Uligon staggered backward, pushing through the guards. One of the guards took his place at the display case, ripping it from the pedestal. Both Uligon and the guard bearing the Eye of Rab'di ran in different directions.

The burly man, however, focused on Uligon. He hurled the shimmering sword like a javelin. The magical blade passed perfectly between the guards around the pedestal, striking Uligon in the small of his back.

Uligon screamed, falling forward. He crashed face-first on the floor. Still screaming, he struggled to crawl away, his limp legs trailing behind him.

A grin formed on Tilthan's face, but he returned his attention to the guard carrying the Eye of Rab'di. The guard soon disappeared.

"After him!" Tilthan whispered, climbing over the railing.

As Tilthan swiftly descended, a battle broke out between the burly man and the guards. The guards struggled to hold their own against their foe. They were repulsed in a manner unlike anything Tilthan had beheld.

The burly man struck with such speed that Tilthan couldn't catch half of his movements. Cornar and his men were skilled fighters, but they were nothing like this.

Tilthan bolted toward the doors leading to where the guard carrying the Eye had fled. Several guards ran through the door, and Tilthan wove around them.

Once at the doors, Tilthan took one final look at the burly man. He held Sire Duarin up by one hand and stared into the Sire's eyes with probing intent.

Nath and Nemral dashed toward the doors, and the three of them hurried through the corridor, following the call for reinforcements—undoubtedly shouted by the man carrying the Eye of Rab'di.

More guards dashed toward them, hurrying to the audience chamber. Tilthan and the others, however, dodged their advance with finesse.

———◦———

Uligon struggled to crawl. The sounds of battle resounded through the audience chamber, heightening his
already frantic mind.

Move!

He couldn't feel anything below his waist.

Struggling, Uligon pulled himself across the floor. He
glanced over his shoulder. That shimmering blade stuck
out of his back. His eyes went wide as his gaze fell upon
the *monster*. The Beast relentlessly seized guard after guard.
Men were frozen in place, and some were decapitated by
their own weapons. More guards hurried into the audience
chamber, advancing on the monstrous intruder.

I have to flee!

A contingent of guards dashed through the audience
chamber's main doors, ten all in all.

"Help!" Uligon cried.

Two of the armor-clad men stopped beside Uligon
while the rest advanced with weapons drawn.

"Your Grace," gasped one of the guards, staring at the
glowing magic protruding from Uligon's back.

"Get me out of here," Uligon pled.

Both guardsmen hefted Uligon onto their shoulders,
hurriedly dragging him toward the doors.

I need an arpranist, Uligon thought. But most of the
arpranists he knew had died or disappeared during the recent slew of murders. *Perhaps—*

A flash of dark green burst beside Uligon, and the
guards carrying him jolted backward. Uligon fell to the
floor. His would-be-rescuers screamed with fright, their

wails fading behind him.

Horror spread across Uligon's face, but he continued to the door, crawling as best he could.

"Enough!" a bellowing cry echoed through the chamber.

A flash of gray light reflected off the walls. But Uligon didn't dare look to its source.

Suddenly, all was quiet.

No! Fear permeated every fiber of his being.

Uligon was almost to the doors when something pinned him in place, but he couldn't feel what.

"You will not flee, abominable qui'sha," a voice declared above Uligon. There was wrath in those words, an unquenchable fury. Horrified, Uligon glanced over his shoulder. The monster retrieved his glowing weapon from Uligon's back, twirling it once in a casual manner.

He knows what I am... Uligon shuddered. That could mean only one thing—

A hand gripped Uligon's shoulder and flipped him over. As he landed on his back, his eyed the monstrous intruder—the one many assumed was Tefan the Headless.

"You," the word oozed with contempt from the monster as he gripped Uligon's throat. "I *hate* you, and your kind. You defile humanity, driving them down erroneous paths that lead to death and destruction. You are the filth of Kalda, the blight of this world!"

Uligon trembled, watching his captor with horror. Those eyes... the vibrant blue irises *swirled* around his captor's pupils.

Not the eyes—

Suddenly, Uligon froze. Vivid memories flashed through

his mind, and he relived all four hundred years of his life. The vision culminated in his more recent memories concerning the Eye of Rab'di and his agreement with Chernil.

You will die too, I fear, Uligon thought. *Oh, Lord Cheserith, receive my soul!*

"What a clever attempt," the monster said with a chuckle. "But this *heist* will be for naught."

Uligon felt control over his mind once again, and he blinked frantically. "Yo-you," he stammered, "you platinum beast!"

The monster grimaced, relinquishing his grip on Uligon.

Uligon fell helplessly as the shimmering sword raced toward him. He watched with horror as the blade flashed toward his neck. His vision spun, and then, all went black.

Tilthan and the others rounded a corner, heavy footfalls echoing off the walls ahead of them. Five guards bounded toward them, several carrying crossbows.

Perfect, Tilthan thought, eyeing the crossbowman on the right. He signed a quick command to Nath and Nemral, telling them to slay the approaching guards. He then drew his dagger.

Within seconds, Tilthan and his troupe clashed with the reinforcements.

Tilthan tackled the crossbowman, stabbing his dagger into the joint between the man's breastplate and pauldron. The crossbowman staggered, but turned about, looking for his assailant.

"Where are they?" blurted one of the guards, swinging

his side-sword blindly.

Tilthan rebounded, swiftly stabbing the other joint. The blow debilitated the crossbowman, causing him to drop his weapon. Tilthan spun, stabbing at the exposed rear thigh of his foe.

Out of the corner of his eye, Tilthan glimpsed his fellow invisible thieves leveling their first foes and advancing on the remaining guards. The last two guardsmen swung wildly, but Nath and Nemral dispatched them with ease. Though the guards wore heavy plate, the thieves managed to land devastating blows into the seams of their armor.

Soon, the patrol of guards had fallen, bleeding from their wounds.

"Do we kill them?" Nemral signed, gesturing to his fallen foe's helmet.

Tilthan shook his head, grabbing the crossbow and several extra bolts. The weapon and the ammo vanished upon his touch.

Another patrol of guards rounded the corner, seeing the carnage wrought by Tilthan and his gang. The guards stopped, glancing nervously about the hall.

"Weave around them," Nath signed, grabbing a crossbow.

The patrol approached warily, and the thieves picked their way around them.

Once Tilthan turned the corner, he dashed down the hall. He turned another corner, coming to a large curving stairwell leading to the lower floors. Clanking footfalls echoed up the stairwell.

He's making good time, Tilthan thought, hurrying down the stairs. *But not good enough.*

Three guards ran from the foot of the steps, one carrying the display case. They hurried out of the room with the stairs, moving into another corridor.

That hall is long, Tilthan thought, recalling the palace's layout. They were still one floor above the vault.

Tilthan leapt from the last step, chasing after his quarry. As he entered the corridor Tilthan steadied himself and aimed the crossbow. The guards were most of the way down the hall, about seventy phineals away.

He aimed at the guard carrying the Eye, focusing on the guard's exposed rear thigh. At this distance it would be a tricky spot to hit, especially with the target moving.

Tilthan fired the bolt, and the guard carrying the Eye fell forward, dropping the display case.

Too easy. He grinned, sprinting briefly while reloading the crossbow. He steadied himself again as Nath and Nemral dashed past, both carrying crossbows.

"Left," Tilthan said flatly, telling which side of the hall he wanted them to run along. He took aim at the next guard, who had just grabbed the display case. As the guard resumed his dash, Tilthan felled him like the first.

One left, he thought, dashing down the hall as he reloaded. The third guard went for the display case.

Nemral unleashed a bolt, but it bounced off the guard's armor. Nath, however, fired a bolt, felling the guard.

"Gotta work on your aim," Tilthan signed, grinning at Nemral as he passed.

Nemral was not amused.

The guards yelled for reinforcements and struggled to stand.

Tilthan and the others reached them quickly. "We

should kill these," he signed, then reached for the nearest guard's helmet. He managed an opening, then slammed his dagger into the man's neck. Both Nath and Nemral did the same, and the corridor fell silent.

The three thieves gathered around the display case and the glowing Eye of Rab'di. The case was on its side, exposing its base. The bottom was completely flat.

"Let's carry this away," Tilthan signed.

Nath picked up the display case, his touch veiling the case with concealing magic.

At that moment, more guards filled the corridor behind them.

Tilthan led the others down the hall, rounding another corner and evading the reinforcements.

It wasn't long before they found a secluded spot.

"That was close," Nemral signed.

Nath nodded, still holding the display case.

Tilthan, however, maneuvered toward the case, examining it. There were no other magical emissions, besides what came from the Eye of Rab'di. Even if there was a tevisral-powered trap, Tilthan would have seen a faint glimmer amid the Eye of Rab'di's glowing aura.

"Do we just break it?" Nemral signed.

Tilthan ignored him, and pulled gently on the base. It didn't budge. He searched the bottom for any seams, but found nothing.

"You're being too meticulous, Tilthan," Nemral signed.

Again, Tilthan ignored Nemral. Throughout his many adventures, Tilthan had learned one couldn't be too careful when stealing something of value. The ancients loved to trap precious things, and it was a custom many modern peoples adopted.

"Set it down, Nath," Nemral said, moving down the hall. He hefted his crossbow, loading another bolt.

Nath complied, hurrying away as Nemral aimed at the now visible display case.

"Wait!" Tilthan signed frantically. But it was too late.

Nemral pulled the trigger and a bolt flew from the crossbow

Tilthan leapt backward, nearly stumbling over himself. Glass shattered before he could regain his footing. "You idiot!" Tilthan signed, glaring at Nemral. "There *could* have been a fatal trap in that base."

Lowering the crossbow, Nemral grinned. "You're fine," he whispered. "Now, let's get out of here before Tefan comes looking for our heads."

Nath hurried back to the broken display case, snatching the large Eye of Rab'di. He tossed it into his pack.

At that moment, Tilthan heard faint footfalls approaching, followed by a faint observation. "...came from this way!"

Tilthan gave Nemral a sullen look, but it didn't last long.

All three thieves hurried out of their hiding spot, narrowly evading a patrol of guards.

7

GETAWAY

But as to how this prophecy will come to pass, I do not know. Not even the qui'sha I have probed know.

Two sets of patrols hurried past Tilthan and the other thieves; the guards had undoubtedly heard Nemral's blundering. *I'm gonna have to work on him,* Tilthan thought, glancing to Nemral. The thief still held the crossbow.

"There is a staircase past the next corridor," Nath signed awkwardly, using only one hand.

"Can't we go any faster?" Nemral signed, looking nervous, his signs more awkward than Nath's.

Tilthan drew his lips to a line, but didn't answer. They were already walking briskly, as fast as Tilthan felt comfortable when sneaking.

They turned a corner, seeing a long hallway with three corridors branching to the left. Tilthan could barely see a large room at the far end with a curved stairwell. It looked identical to the stairs where they had chased the guards.

As they were partway down the corridor, an abrupt cry resounded from whence they had come.

Tilthan glanced over his shoulder, but kept moving.

A shout soon followed, accompanied by the clash of metal against stone.

"It's him…" Nemral muttered, his fear apparent.

"Hush!" Tilthan signed harshly. The damned fool was going to give them away. *You idiot, Nem! Just be quiet!*

Footsteps and clinking armor came from ahead, echoing from one of the side corridors. Soon, a patrol of guards rounded the corner.

"Did you hear that?" asked the lead guard.

The others nodded.

"It sounded like it came from that way," another guard said, pointing in the direction of Tilthan and the others.

"Someone is probably after that rock," the lead guard said, hurrying toward the thieves.

Tilthan and his compatriots pressed themselves to the walls, and the guards passed by in twos. While Tilthan watched the guards pass, another figure entered the hallway. It was that burly man.

"Halt!" the guards shouted in unison. "By command of the Korathi Royal Guard, halt!"

"Tefan…" Nemral muttered, but the guards didn't seem to hear him.

"Run!" Nath gritted through clenched teeth.

The faint pitter-patter of Nath and Nemral's dashing feet faded while Tilthan eyed the burly man. *Tefan the Headless?* Tilthan wondered. Could this man really be a ghost—?

Tefan averted his gaze from the guards, looking right at

Tilthan. Startled, Tilthan spun and ran after his friends. *Did he really look at me?* he thought, aghast.

The sounds of a swift skirmish filled the hall behind Tilthan, but it abruptly ceased. Had that Tefan killed the entire patrol?

As Tilthan neared the foot of the stairs another patrol rushed past him. They had probably heard the guards' declaration for Tefan—or whoever that was—to halt. A sudden spike of fear shot through Tilthan. *Is he really Tefan?*

Nath and Nemral were already up the stairs when Tilthan began his climb. The two thieves were running faster than ever before. Tilthan could barely keep up with them.

The thieves hurried through corridor after corridor. But no matter how far they ran, a cacophony of chaos trailed after them. They passed several patrols, but each hurried past, shouting "halt" to Tefan. After the fourth patrol, Tilthan glanced over his shoulder. The burly man engaged the guards in a swift melee, but somehow Tefan froze the guards whenever he looked at them—rather, when the guards looked at him.

Could ghosts *freeze* people? Tilthan didn't remember that being attributed to apparitions.

Eventually—as they reached the building housing the servants' quarters—Tilthan caught up to Nath and Nemral.

"He's after us!" Nemral gritted through clenched teeth. "Tefan wants our heads!"

Nath glanced to Nemral, the expression on his face showed that he agreed.

"He can see us," Tilthan signed, but only Nath saw it.

"How?" Nath mouthed.

Tilthan shrugged as they ran. They turned a corner, entering a curved hall with floor-to-ceiling windows. A nearby bridge led to the palace's outer wall. Rain pelted the windows while an occasional flash of lightning lit the darkened clouds; the booming thunder was faint. The rain would definitely reveal them.

Another cry of "Intruder!" echoed behind the thieves.

We sure are getting lucky with all these patrols, Tilthan thought. He feared what would have happened if the palace guard hadn't been around. Tefan would have caught them and claimed their heads. *You're thinking like Nem*, Tilthan chided himself. Perhaps it was the fear that made him believe, and the swiftness at which Tefan dispatched the guards. No living thing could do that...

As they passed the last window, the corridor straightened. The double doors leading to the bridge—guarded by two armored men—lay not far ahead. Both guards spun, readying their weapons. They had undoubtedly heard the dashing footfalls.

"I don't see any—" The guard cut himself short, his eyes widening as he gazed beyond the invisible thieves. "You there, halt!"

He's right behind us! Tilthan didn't dare look.

Both guards moved into the hall and the thieves wove around them, throwing the doors open. The guards outside on the bridge started and spun, but they didn't seem to notice the thieves, despite the heavy rain pelting Tilthan and his comrades.

As the thieves ran across the bridge, Tilthan heard splashes and clinking armor fading into the palace. He didn't dare peek.

There was, however, another patrol on the ramparts. The guards looked toward the bridge, but their eyes were drawn to the open doors. They hurried into the tower between them and the bridge.

"We have to hurry," Tilthan signed, but neither of his friends was paying attention. They dashed up the stairs leading to the palace's ramparts as the patrol emerged from the tower.

Tilthan stifled a curse. The guards would undoubtedly see three outlines where the rain abruptly stopped. Most men knew what that meant.

One of the guards squinted toward Tilthan and the others, but was drawn by a cry from the leader. "You on the bridge, halt!" All but the squinting guard hurried past the invisible thieves, dashing down the stairs. The lone guard continued squinting into the rain, readying his fanisar.

Tilthan drew his dagger, but as the blade left his sheath a whizzing bolt raced beside him from behind. The projectile became visible, striking the seam between the guard's breastplate and pauldron.

Good shot, Tilthan thought, advancing swiftly.

The guard reeled, swinging his fanisar toward Tilthan. "Intruders on the ram—"

Tilthan evaded the weapon. He punched the guard's upper chest, knocking him off balance. The guard hit the inner balustrade, and Tilthan sliced his foe's exposed hamstring—a debilitating blow.

Peeling away, Tilthan glanced to the bridge. Tefan had engaged the patrol and his hands were glowing with pale-gray light, and his touch seemed to still all. It reminded

Tilthan of how Iltar mesmerized monsters while out adventuring.

He can't be a ghost... Tilthan thought.

Nath and Nemral were already climbing over the parapet, descending ropes secured to the wall by climbing
hooks.

Tilthan didn't skip a beat, and swiftly removed his own
rope. He held the knot with one hand and threw the hook
with the other, then leapt over the wall. The hook caught
as he plummeted, the recoil jolting him. Tilthan hit the
wall, but regained control, swiftly rappelling to the ground.

Above him, the sounds of battle ceased.

Nath and Nemral landed as Tilthan tugged on his rope,
freeing his climbing hook.

"Better hurry, boys," Tilthan whispered, coiling the rope
around his elbow.

The other thieves tugged their ropes and ran, dragging
the hooks behind them.

Tilthan cursed under his breath, then hurried after his
friends. They frantically coiled the ropes as they ran.

"The drain is up ahead," Nath hollered. "North of the
reservoir."

"What?" Tilthan blurted, winding the last of his rope.
There was no drain in their escape plan.

"A backup, Tilthan," Nath shouted.

They passed the reservoir, coming upon a hole in the
ground. A metal grate was pulled aside. Acrid fumes as-
sailed Tilthan's nostrils, accompanied by the faint sound of
flowing water.

A sewer? The thought of swimming in waste disgusted
Tilthan, but it was better than the alternative.

Something crashed behind them. Tilthan dared a glance as Nath dropped into the hole.

Tefan rose from the ground, gazing at them—like a lion stalking his prey. Had he leapt five stories and remained unscathed? How was that possible?

"Come on!" Nemral shouted, his voice vanishing into the stench.

Tilthan shook his head as he leapt into the hole. All the while, he heard a bellowing voice behind him. "You can't run forever." The words faded as a putrid current swept Tilthan into a nauseating abyss.

Tilthan slid for what seemed an eternity. Filthy liquid splashed his face, dousing his nostrils in the worst smells imaginable. He fought the urge to vomit, but he could feel the bile welling in his throat.

It was pure torment.

Suddenly, he felt himself falling. Tilthan struck the surface of a disgusting pool, then became submerged. He had no time to catch his breath, but he didn't want to inhale the acrid air. Frantically, he swam upward.

As Tilthan cleared the putrid surface, noxious liquid spewed from his mouth.

Nemral popped up next to him, retching. "Well," he said when he could speak, "I've never done that before."

"I hope I never do it again," Tilthan croaked. He blinked several times, noticing pinhole streams of moonlight above him.

"At least we're alive," Nath chimed.

Tilthan grumbled. "Always the optimist…"

"Where are we?" Nemral asked.

"Probably someplace by the shore," Nath said, his voice accompanied by splashing. "There's a ledge over here."

"You don't think Tefan is behind us, do you?" Nemral asked.

"I hope not," Nath said, and climbed onto the ledge. "Do ghosts fear feces?"

Tilthan's eyes gradually adjusted to the darkness. From what he could tell, they were in a large space, probably half the size of a city block. The ceiling looked to be a floor and a half above them. Most of the city's waste probably flowed to this place.

"Over here," Nath said, beckoning through the gloom.

Tilthan and Nemral swam to the ledge. Tilthan fought the urge to vomit again as he touched *things* floating in the vile pool. He felt relieved once he reached the ledge.

"This way," Nath gestured, moving along the ledge. "I see a ladder."

Within seconds, they were all up the ladder and in a less putrid corridor of plainly hewn stone. It was probably an overflow duct.

"How do you suppose he could see us?" Nath asked as they walked.

Tilthan shook his head. "I saw no tevisrals on him." He didn't know of any other way of seeing through invisibility.

"He's a ghost," Nemral said matter-of-factly. "They can see through magic…" The thief let the thought linger before continuing. "How many heads do you think he took tonight? The death toll must be in the thousands!"

"I don't know…" Nath said thoughtfully. "I think what we encountered was something different from a ghost."

"If it was the Headless, wouldn't he be lacking a head?" Tilthan asked rhetorically. Whoever it was pursuing them had a head, and a functional one at that.

"Perhaps he possessed someone, you know?" Nemral interjected. "That would explain why he was able to interact with the guards."

Nath didn't look convinced.

They continued debating the nature of Tefan as they searched for a way out of the sewers. Eventually, they came to another ladder leading to a grate. Soon, the thieves were on the streets of the lower city. The fresh air was a welcome relief.

Tilthan felt as if he had ascended from the depths of damnation itself. He stretched his arms wide, embracing the rain. The purifying rain.

"Looks like we're by the docking district," Nemral signed. "We should hurry."

With his arms still wide, Tilthan looked about. They were near the western borders of Korath. The cliffs where the palace stood were perhaps several grand phineals away.

Nemral began to move, but stopped when he noticed Tilthan still standing in the rain. "What are you doing?" he signed.

"I'm cleansing myself," Tilthan replied.

"You're going to need a more thorough cleaning than that," Nath signed, a wry grin on his face. "I doubt your rain bath will be sufficient to attract any company tonight."

Tilthan pouted, not amused by his friend's jest. Nath,

however, was grinning widely.

Putting his arms down, Tilthan stalked through the street. "Let's get back to our employer," he signed. The sooner they could finish this job, the better.

8

PAYMENT

Nevertheless, the prophecies of Cherisium have proven accu-
rate. This is why I am fearful of the Au'misha'k.

Despite traveling through the rain, Tilthan still stank. It had taken him and his fellow thieves two hours to reach the Cliffside Vista. During that time the rain had intensified. Hardly anyone was outside, but the thieves clung to the shadows as if they were visible—they practically were in the rain.

Tilthan called for a halt as they neared the inn, then gestured to a nearby alleyway. "Nem, take your cloak off," he signed the command.

"Why me?" Nemral demanded, looking about warily. The encounter with Tefan was still fresh in his mind.

"Because I'm the leader," Tilthan signed.

Nemral grumbled, removing his cloak. As he appeared, he stuffed the shimmering shroud into his pack, and then tucked his thieving lenses into the inner pocket of his tunic. Once his things were secured, Nemral led them back into the street.

Retarin was outside, smoking his pipe. Two more of Chernil's guards—Tilthan couldn't remember their names—stood with Retarin. At first glance their congregating in the rain looked rather odd; but then again, there weren't many passersby to question the choice in venue. Retarin nodded as Nemral approached, but then flinched with disgust.

"What's that stench?" Retarin griped, choking on his pipe.

One of the men sneered. "It's foul…"

"We accidently fell into a sewer," Nemral said with a shrug.

The bodyguards frowned with disgust, but led the thieves inside nonetheless.

Those in the foyer of the Cliffside Vista flinched as Tilthan and the others entered. It was oddly satisfying to Tilthan. If he had to bear the stench, it was only fair that others shared his burden.

As before, Retarin led the thieves to Chernil's suite. But this time his pace was quicker. He threw the doors open, muttering.

Nemral led the way inside, but the guards lingered in the hall. The door swung shut as Nemral entered the common room.

"You're back!" Chernil cheered, his voice echoing into the suite's foyer. But his cheers abruptly turned to coughing. "You… smell."

Grinning, Tilthan unlatched only the clasp generating his invisible veil. Nath did the same.

"We had to take a detour," Tilthan said, placing his

hands on his hips.

Chernil writhed in his chair, making a disgusted face. He spat his keav back into his wineglass. "You should have bathed before coming here!" Chernil coughed and fanned the air with his hand, attempting to swat the stench away.

"Well, time is of the essence," Tilthan continued. "We were running from a ghost, after all."

Mocking laughter left Chernil's lips. "You... you are an idiot, Tilthan."

"Tell that to all the dead guards in the palace," Nemral said. He removed his cloak from his sack, latching only one of the clasps.

All three thieves were prepared to vanish. Not that it mattered, since Tefan could see them somehow. That, and the rain.

"Dead guards?" Chernil's disgust became confusion.

"Yeah," Tilthan nodded. "Seems you aren't the only one who wants that Eye-thing. What with it being a tevisral and all."

Chernil's face went bleak.

So, he does know, Tilthan thought. *Well, in that case we better renegotiate the deal.*

"Not to mention we almost died," Nemral chimed. "Tefan. Tefan the Headless. He cut down the palace guards like blades of grass. He froze men in place with his gaze and passed through solid glass. We barely escaped with our lives."

Chernil's eyes went wide.

One of Chernil's bodyguards entered the common room, carrying another bottle of keav. Xlyar, was it?

"And I think your friend is dead," Nath interjected.

"Tefan stabbed him in the back."

Chernil flinched. "Did... did this *Tefan* seize him?"

Tilthan didn't know the answer to that question. It was possible that Uligon had gotten away. But Tilthan doubted a crawling man could outrun something such as Tefan.

"I don't know," Nath shrugged. "Why?"

"He must have..." Nemral said shakily, "I mean, Tefan moved so fast. We barely escaped, even running as fast as we could."

Chernil's face paled, and he turned to Xlyar. "Gather the others. We must leave immediately."

"Oh, now wait a minute!" Tilthan said. "We have some negotiating ahead of us. When you hired us, we agreed on a rate for a rock, a big shiny rock, but a rock nonetheless. Things are different now that we *know it's a tevisral.*" Tilthan emphasized the last bit, hoping to impress that he had deduced Chernil's plans for the Eye.

"It's not a tevisral!" Chernil snarled. "Just a component to one, a power source. Retarin," he shouted toward the foyer, "get in here!"

A component? Tilthan thought. But weren't things like that supposed to be tiny? What kind of tevisral required something the size of the Eye of Rab'di? The very idea made his mind spin with possibilities.

The doors swung open, and the three bodyguards entered, holding their forearms to their noses.

"We leave immediately!" Chernil commanded.

They nodded and hurried off to the other rooms.

Tilthan glanced to his fellow thieves, noticing Nath signing discretely.

"What do we do now?" After Nath signed the question

he patted his sack.

Tilthan was about to reply when Chernil spoke. "We can debate payment later, once we are safely aboard my ship."

"You mean you didn't bring our payment?" Tilthan demanded. He didn't like the idea of traveling with Chernil. He had hoped to get paid and make a return trip to Soroth through the Kingdom of Los.

Chernil coughed and warded the putrid odor with his hand. "No. Do you take me for a fool?"

Tilthan tensed at the question.

"Now, hand *it* over," Chernil gestured with an outstretched hand. "You have it, don't you?" He pressed the question through clenched teeth.

The thieves glanced to each other, and Tilthan nodded.

Reluctantly, Nath removed the crimson sphere from his pack. The Eye of Rab'di glowed brighter than any other lightstone in the room. Its aura was cast on the walls—an effect Tilthan hadn't seen within the palace. *Beautiful*, he thought.

Chernil snatched the Eye from Nath, grinning widely. He was closer to the thieves now, and their stench—but that didn't seem to bother him.

"Finally," Chernil muttered. "We can finish—" He cut off abruptly, pursing his lips to a line. Wary, Chernil stepped back from the thieves, then shouted for one of his bodyguards to retrieve something for him to secure the Eye.

"So, do you have *anything* on you?" Nemral asked. "I mean, of our payment."

Still holding the Eye of Rab'di, Chernil glanced to

Nemral, but his expression turned ghastly.

Tilthan followed Chernil's gaze, his eyes drawn to a pale brown-gray tint on the nearest window. *Magic?* he thought, then flinched. *It's him—*

A flash of black flew from the eaves and *through* the hued glass. Tefan. The ghost, man, mage, or whatever he was, landed and rebounded with grace; his veil of invisibility departed from him, but he still glowed with enhancing magic.

Chernil screamed, then stumbled away as his guards re-entered the common room. They drew their weapons, pushing aside furniture as they rushed Tefan.

Tilthan was so perplexed that he couldn't move. How had Tefan found them? *This is no man*, Tilthan thought.

With his hand still imbued with enthralling power, Tefan engaged all seven bodyguards, swiftly immobilizing them while muttering some sharp-sounding gibberish.

Green light shot from Tefan, racing toward Chernil.

Impossible! Tilthan balked, his eyes wide. *That couldn't have been an incantation. It couldn't!*

The green light became enthralling tentacles that caught Chernil short of the suite's doors.

"Come!" Tefan barked, making a pulling gesture that whipped Chernil from the foyer.

Chernil—suspended in front of Tefan by the tentacles—dropped the Eye, and it rolled back into the common room, stopping not far from Nath. The thief glanced at the crimson sphere, but didn't move.

Nemral didn't move either.

Tilthan shot a quick glance to the window, the same one Tefan had passed through. It was still glowing that pale brown-gray hue.

I could jump through it, he thought. Tilthan imagined his escape, freeing his climbing hook as he fell and catching it on a rooftop. The fall would be fatal if he missed. He wouldn't miss. He *couldn't* miss.

But could the others duplicate the feat? His friends were not as skilled... And, there was no way for Tilthan to share his plan. Sure, he would pass in front of Nemral—hopefully that would jar the thief from his stupor. But Nath. Well, Tilthan would have to get his attention, and fast.

"Nath..." Tilthan breathed.

Tefan ignored the whisper, gazing into Chernil's eyes. Nath, however, turned.

As their eyes met, Tilthan darted for the window. He *threw* himself at the glass and went *through* it. Passing through the window was like leaping through a waterfall, though he didn't feel wet. He hit the balcony's railing and it gave way against him. But as Tilthan fell beyond the balcony he stopped, dangling in the air. Something wrapped around him, pulling his arms to his sides. His legs also clamped together.

"What on Kalda—"

Tilthan flew backward into the common room.

"You cannot flee," Tefan said, turning from Chernil. "I must know if you are *defiled*."

Defiled? Tilthan thought, aghast. "Uh, what kind of *defiling* are we talking about?" he asked nervously. A few perverse ideas ran through his head. *Yuck!*

With that, Tefan uttered more gibberish, and a shimmering shaft of light resembling a sword appeared in his hand. He swiftly spun, decapitating Chernil. The tentacles holding Chernil's headless body dissipated, and the corpse fell.

"I better not be defiled!" Tilthan lamented. At that moment, he was glad Sharon hadn't accompanied them. *At least she's safe*, he thought.

Tefan moved through the room, staring into the eyes of Chernil's bodyguards. One by one he slew each, decapitating them. Nath and Nemral, however, remained paralyzed.

"Behold," Tefan said, gesturing to the headless corpses, "the fate of the defiled." He stepped toward Tilthan. "This is their reward for walking erroneous paths and perpetuating dangerous ideals. The defiled must be *cleansed* from Kalda if we are to prevent another Thousand Years War."

Tilthan stared at Tefan with wide eyes. What did that even mean? Confused, he averted his gaze, looking past the murderous madman. Nath was now gawking wide-eyed at the headless corpses, as if the sight were something new to him. Tilthan followed Nath's gaze while wondering, *What are you—?* He started, staring at his dead employer. But what lay where Chernil was slain was *not* Chernil. It wasn't even human!

The severed head was covered in crimson scales. Where the mouth and nose should have been was an elongated snout that bore sharp teeth. There was no hair, nor skin anywhere on that head.

Tilthan stared with horror at that head, even as Tefan spoke.

"If you wish to save yourself, you must look into my eyes. It is the only way I can discern your purity."

Look into his eyes? Tilthan thought, slowly turning from

the bizarre head. He focused on Tefan. Tilthan started upon seeing Tefan's eyes—the brilliant blue irises swirled in a pattern *around* his pupils. Flecks of red and black were also in that swirling pattern. Those eyes were inhuman.

What manner of eyes—?

Suddenly, Tilthan lost control of everything. His entire life flashed before him. He relived his boyhood pranks with his friends, the heartache of his youth, and lucrative adventures across the world. But amid those memories were flashes of Demitru.

Why Demitru?

One memory in particular stood out, one Tilthan had all but forgotten. He and Demitru had been in Klath, about ten years ago. Demitru insisted on making an introduction to several friends of his, but Tilthan declined, as he was due to meet Uncle Cedath in preparation for a forthcoming adventure with Iltar and Cornar. Then, a line from Demitru jumped out at him. "Tilthan, you *have* to meet Delar. After an hour with him, you will never see the world the same." More memories flashed in Tilthan's mind, all leading up to stealing the Eye of Rab'di.

Then, the visions faded.

Tilthan blinked and shook his head.

"You are not defiled," Tefan said, waving his hand in a dismissal.

The tentacles around Tilthan slithered away, and he fell to the floor. "Geez, thanks," he said unsteadily.

Tefan then moved onto Nemral. He stared into the thief's eyes for only a moment.

Had it been that short? Tilthan wondered. It felt as if he lived a lifetime during the stare-down with Tefan. Nemral had probably relived his entire life, too.

"You are not defiled, either," Tefan said, spinning from Nemral. He then strode to Nath and stared into his eyes.

"Good," Tefan said, "you are not defiled, either." There was a long pause before he spoke again. "I tire of killing men."

Nath gasped, looking around the room as if to gain his bearings.

"I would be tired too if I killed a thousand men," Nemral muttered. "That's how many you killed in Korath, wasn't it?"

"Three hundred and nine," Tefan said with a frown. "The other hundred and forty-three were qui'sha."

"They were what?" Tilthan muttered.

Tefan simply pointed to the not-Chernil corpse. "He was qui'sha. I am surprised at how many were here in Korath. There were not so many in Karbenath." He knelt beside Chernil's scaled corpse, then whispered something. Suddenly, violet light appeared in his hand.

Disintegrating magic? Tilthan wondered, watching as the violet light shot to the scaled corpse. It was gone within seconds, as if it were never there.

Tilthan gawked in amazement. *How can he muster magic so fast?*

Tefan shook his hand and the disintegrating aura dissipated. "These things corrupt our world," he said, moving toward the Eye of Rab'di. "The byproduct of a mad god."

"Uh"—Tilthan cleared his throat—"are you going to take that?"

Tefan turned, glancing at Tilthan with a raised brow before picking up the Eye. He did not look amused. "What uses have you for an ul'sil'em?"

Tilthan furrowed his brow, then shrugged. "Um, I could sell it?"

Nath struck his head against his open palm, looking embarrassed.

"What?" Tilthan asked. It was an honest answer.

A grin formed across Tefan's stony face. "I like you, Tilthan. Always the opportunist." He hefted the crimson sphere. "No, I fear I cannot give this to you. An ul'sil'em in the wrong hands could prove disastrous."

"Can we at least keep their stuff?" Tilthan gestured to the corpses. "We were never paid in full for completing our job."

Tefan crossed the room, his grin fading. "If you must…" He walked to the windows but before he moved through the glass, Nemral muttered a question.

"Are you really Tefan the Headless? The vengeful ghost?"

Tefan chuckled. "A ghost? No… I am very much alive. But, Tefan… I have not gone by that name in a long, long time."

With that, Tefan uttered a single sharp word, "Sium," and a veil of concealing magic engulfed him.

Tilthan gawked. *But that was no incantation!* He stared, watching Tefan move *through* the window and then leap unnaturally to the roof. If Tefan landed, Tilthan didn't hear it.

The thieves stood silently for a while, until Nemral finally spoke. "I can't believe we're alive."

"We're lucky," Nath exclaimed, "Lucky! Perhaps even more than Hemrin!" He burst into laughter.

Soon, all three of them were laughing. As their mirth died, Tilthan stood. "Well, boys," he said, "let's pick this place clean. And then let's find ourselves a bath!"

9

SWEET PARTING

So, I implore you—destroy it! If I knew where the Keepers had secreted it, I would go myself and banish it from our world.

Unfortunately, Chernil and his thugs traveled rather light. They carried some gold coins and a few trinkets. Most of the coins were from Comdolith, but some of them had apparently been exchanged for chilgins—the predominate form of currency on the Isle of Korath.

Disappointed, the thieves returned to The Fairy and the Drake. No one besides the assistant innkeeper was awake. It was the middle of the night, after all. Still invisible, the thieves crept into the men's common bath at the back of the inn.

Inside the large room, twelve bronze tubs lined the walls. A pair of hand pumps stood beside each tub. One pumped water from the city's aqueducts. The other pumped water from a large black cauldron—big enough to fit three men—situated at the far side of the room. The cauldron was suspended above a dormant fire pit.

"Well, boys," Tilthan said, unlatching his cloak, "let's clean our things. Nem, get a fire going."

Nath began pumping to fill the large cauldron while Tilthan grabbed the soap—it was the lightest of the tasks, after all. Nemral's job wasn't that bad either, as the cauldron was often filled with water, to some degree.

Soon, a fire roared beneath the enormous black cauldron. When its water was steaming, Nemral and Nath moved to the pumps beside the tubs.

"Aren't you going to help?" Nath grumbled.

Tilthan blinked innocently. "Who, me?"

Nath rolled his eyes.

"Okay, fine…" Tilthan sighed.

After half an hour, the tubs were finally filled. Nemral checked on the water, and it was lukewarm.

Tilthan, however, didn't want to wait. The stench was unbearable! He immediately stripped off his clothes and threw them into the tub designated for laundry. He threw his pack and tevisrals in as well. Everything had to be cleaned. Everything.

"You know," Nath said, "they're not going to get as clean as they can be without hot water…"

Ignoring his friend, Tilthan scrubbed at his clothes. His shimmering cloak floated above the water, but his spectacles sank to the tub's bottom.

"So, what are we going to do about the rest of our payment?" Nemral asked.

Tilthan focused on scrubbing, but Nath frowned in thought.

"We have that first payment back home," Nemral continued. "And it will go for a lot, probably enough to live off for a year or two after we split it four ways… But I was hoping for more."

"Getting greedy, Nem?" Tilthan said with a chuckle.

Nemral shrugged.

Tilthan knew why he wanted more—Uncle Cedath's royalty fee.

A sigh left Nemral's lips. "I mean, we really don't have enough coin on us to travel back to Soroth. We could probably make it to Klath…"

Nemral had a point. Tilthan had expected Chernil to pay them here, and then they would part ways. It was Tilthan's intent to travel back to Klath and stay there for a while, or until Kadren was in port. He would give them a free ride back to Soroth.

"Let's go back to Chernil's ship," Nath suggested.

"And do what?" Tilthan said, and laughed. "Swipe the rest of our payment?"

Nath nodded. "I doubt anyone will notice if it goes missing. Sure, the ship belonged to Chernil, but do you really think he trusted the captain or his crew with access to those gems?"

Tilthan continued scrubbing. "It sounds risky… If anyone finds out that we took the payment we will be the first suspects. I really don't want a bounty on my head."

"So, steal our payment, and then what?" Nemral asked.

"Make our way to Klath," Nath said. "We can exchange the gems for coin, and ride comfortably home. From Klath we can sail back to Soroth."

Nath and Nemral continued discussing the matter while

Tilthan kept scrubbing. The more he thought about
Nath's plan, the more he thought it might work. But there
was that lingering thought of being caught by Chernil's
associates. If a man like Chernil disappeared, it wouldn't
go unnoticed. And no sane person would let Chernil's
wealth sit around to molder. Eventually, *someone* would
discover that the gems had gone missing, especially when
the Eye of Rab'di was never received.

Then there was Demitru. *We could never mention it to him*,
Tilthan thought.

"What do you say, Tilthan?" Nemral asked.

Tilthan drew his lips to a line, drying his thieving lenses.
He stared at the spectacles for a moment before answer-
ing. "Let's do it," he said in a tone of resignation.

After an hour and a half, the hot water was ready.
Tilthan had since finished cleaning his clothes and his
tevisrals. They hung on a line running the length of the
room.

Nath and Nemral had just begun cleaning their things as
Tilthan eagerly pumped his personal tub with hot water.
After a dozen pumps he tested the bath.

"Just right!" Tilthan exclaimed, leaping into the tub
with a splash.

"You're getting water all over the floor," Nath said flatly, scrubbing his shimmering cloak.

You sound like my mother... Tilthan thought, leaning back
against the tub's wall. "Ahh..." he sighed, "to be clean
again!"

Tilthan and the others finished bathing around first light. They slept most of the day and woke near evening. Not wanting to rush to the evening ferry, Tilthan and the others decided to stay one more night in Korath.

The thieves retired to the inn's tavern for their first meal of the day. The room was already crowded, and the patrons were quite lively, even more so than the night before the heist. The same musicians were playing, but their tunes were more energetic than before.

All the tables were occupied, as were the booths along the wall. That left only the bar, but they couldn't find three seats together.

Tilthan snagged an open stool near the middle, between two rowdy parties. He grinned at the patrons while waiting for the bartender to come near, his eyes moving between the bar and the stage.

Tilthan rather enjoyed the atmosphere of The Fairy and the Drake. Despite its lack of gambling, it was a pleasurable place. *I might have to come back here again*, he thought.

"You ready?" the bartender hollered.

Tilthan turned. A flash of dark brown-almost-black moved beside him. Before he could speak, a woman's voice replied to the bartender.

"He'll have some warm messel," she said, "and I want some ale."

Tilthan turned and grinned. *Oh my...*

Cilara leaned against the counter, facing Tilthan but her brilliant blue eyes were on the bartender.

"Messel wasn't all I intended to order," he said flippantly.

She slowly turned her eyes toward Tilthan, a smug grin

forming on her lips. "He'll be back," she said.

Her pupils are dilated again, he thought, a wry smirk forming on his face.

"Do you have plans tonight?" she asked.

Tilthan shook his head. "I have the *whole* night ahead of me!" he exclaimed.

Cilara's grin grew even wider.

For a while they talked about nothing in particular. The bartender returned with the drinks, and Tilthan ordered a plate of crotu. Eventually, Cilara brought up the theft at the palace.

"Did you hear the Eye of Rab'di was stolen?" she asked.

"Really?" Tilthan feigned ignorance.

"There were some beheadings, too; the chamberlain and a bunch of guards. Then there were several guards who died from stab wounds. And a nobleman disappeared— one of the men who helped organize the tour at the palace." Cilara paused and took a sip from her stein. "It all seems strange. And no one saw anything."

No one? Tilthan thought. But dozens of guards had seen Tefan in the palace. There was even a battle in the audience chamber, for magic's sake! How was it possible that no one had seen him? *He's like a ghost...* Tilthan thought. Although Tefan was alive, his actions marked him otherwise.

"No one saw *anything*?" he asked.

Cilara nodded. "Not a single one... but at least the murders stopped," she added. "The last bodies to be found were at the Cliffside Vista. Seven men, dead. But their rooms were picked clean, so the City Watch thinks someone else might have killed them."

Their conversation devolved into small talk once again as Tilthan's food arrived.

"So, how long are you staying in Korath?" Cilara asked. "You never answered me the other night."

Swallowing his food, Tilthan held up a finger. "We leave in the morning," he replied. "My friends and I have to get back to work."

"Well, that leaves us plenty of time to have fun *tonight*," Cilara said with a sensual grin.

Tilthan eyed her up and down, taking in her beauty. He was rarely with a woman twice—unless it was the morning after. But he would make an exception for Cilara. *It might be rather fun*, Tilthan thought. Besides, he had time to kill before they had to steal their payment from Chernil's ship.

Tefan was a name Chis'ilak had borne ages ago, and he hadn't heard it spoken except in fearful whispers. He felt an odd sense of nostalgia for it. He had seen the world differently as Tefan Anigos. *That was a time of ideals*, he thought, *a time of innocence and blind obedience.* Those were the days when he *hearkened* to the mandate given to him by the Lords of Metal, the Ril'Sha.

But those days were long past.

Wind drew Chis'ilak from his reverie; a sea breeze in the night. It rustled against his face, dampening his skin. The faint glow of the ancient ul'sil'em caught his eye, a glow invisible to the naked *human* eye.

Humans…

Sorrow welled in Chis'ilak's soul. He had slain many men and women over the centuries—none innocent. All were defiled by the Accursed One's doctrine. Those teachings led men to commit abominable acts. Wars were started by men who hearkened to the Accursed One, and to his children—the qui'sha.

None were innocent. Only that fact consoled Chis'ilak.

But then there were some men like Ercanin. *Ercanin.* He played the name over in his mind. Ercanin was a good-hearted man, but defiled nonetheless. His very beliefs could sow the seeds of destruction in generations to come. *That was his only crime, but a crime worthy of death.*

The wind intensified, and Chis'ilak approached rising cliffs overlooking the northern shores of the Isle of Korath. Along the edges of the cliffs stood an old light-house; despite its age, it was well maintained.

Finally. Chis'ilak pursed his lips, the sorrow fading from his heart. *I am home.*

A brilliant lightstone shone bright atop the lighthouse's tower, a beacon for ships sailing toward Karbenath.

Chis'ilak quickened his pace, moving toward a dirt path leading to the lighthouse's entrance. Once at the door he waved his hand. "Vi'sainar cu'las mi'dna xo'rak."

Blue light pulsed across the lighthouse—a barrier of barsion magic, emitted by an array of tevisrals he had placed within the stone exterior. The barsion was a precaution, since he had not tended to the lighthouse in months.

The light faded, and Chis'ilak was inside within seconds. Creaking floorboards marked his path as he moved toward a tight staircase leading to the basement. Sconces covered with dark fabric lined the stairs, but Chis'ilak removed the cloths as he passed.

He wound his way through narrow halls, eventually arriving at a secluded study with no windows. The room was lit by a single lightstone fixture hanging from the ceiling. Tevisrals—great and small alike—rested upon book-shelves; all were outlawed and some were rare beyond measure. They were not his, per se.

Examining the shelves, Chis'ilak cleared a space for the Ul'sil'em and placed the crimson sphere beside a wand and gauntlet. Then, he turned to a small table.

It held a quill and several sheets of parchment as well as several books. The top sheet of parchment had writing upon it, penned by his own hand. "...*But I doubt you will consent to destroying the symbol of our ancestors' victory.*"

Chis'ilak nodded once before sitting. *You decrepit fools must be convinced*, he thought, picking up the quill. *The time is at hand.*

"*I know you will not agree—none of our kind have throughout the ages—but you must be convinced!*" he wrote. "*Destroying it will ensure our Enemy never escapes his prison.*"

Chis'ilak's hand flew across the parchment, urgently penning his innermost fears. Kalda was on the brink of disaster.

"*If you will not hearken to my warning, search the prophecies of our Enemy—particularly the ones recorded by Soron Thahan—and then examine our world over the last thousand years. You will see that all the realms of Kalda are in peril.*"

THE END OF

Companion Story One of
TALES OF THE AMULET

To be continued in...
The Dark Necromancer

GLOSSARY

A glossary of names, people, places, objects, and terms found in *A Thief's Way*. Pronunciations and brief descriptions or definitions included. This glossary contains potential spoilers. Readers beware.

Arpran (are-PRAN): a type, or channel, of magic that can heal, regenerate, and prolong life.

Arpranist (are-PRAN-ist): a mage practicing the arpran magical discipline.

Amulet of Draconic Control: an ancient tevisral created by the Irum'mak'sha toward the end of the Thousand Years War. It had the power to control red dragons. Coupled with the tethering stone, the Amulet could open a one-way portal to other worlds.

Au'misha'k (ow-MI-shaa-k): the draconic name for the Amulet of Draconic Control.

Barsion (BAR-zhi-ON): a type, or channel, of protective magic used primarily to create defensive barriers, but it can also restrain.

Brandleberry (bran-DULL-berry): a tart berry native to Kalda. It is often juiced and fermented into a wine.

Cedath (cee-DAHTH): the man who taught Tilthan, Nath and Nemral their thieving trade. Tilthan's great uncle.

Chernil (CHUR-nill): an aristocratic and wealthy man who hired Tilthan and his thieving troupe. He is an associate of Tilthan's friend, Demitru.

Cherisium (cher-IS-ee-UM): a prominent religion dating back to the Karthar Empire.

Chis'ilak (chiss-IL-ack): a draconic name meaning; "born for justice."

Cilara (sil-aura): a woman from Korath trained as a historian and well versed in art.

City Watch: a civil organization within most cities devoted to keeping the peace.

Cliffside Vista: a inn in the city of Korath

Colvin brandy (cole-vin): a type of strong alcohol, green in color.

Cornar (CORE-nahr): a notorious warrior and adventurer. His signature weapons are a double-bladed short sword and a serrated dagger.

Crotu (crow-TOO): a fish native to the Sea of Korath with yellow flesh. When filleted and cooked, crotu has a golden coloring.

Delar (DEL-aar): an associate of Demitru.

Demitru (deh-MEE-true): a childhood friend of Tilthan, Nath, and Nemral. He received one of three sets of thieving tevisrals gifted to Tilthan by Cedath. Demitru opted not to join Tilthan's thieving troupe.

Devout(s): a term used to describe anyone who ascribes to the Cherisium religion.

Dorin (dore-EN): the first king of the Kingdom of Los, also known as Dorin the Mage-King. He wielded a weapon called, "The King's Scepter." The men of Los often curse "by Dorin's Scepter."

Duarin (doo-rin): a nobleman of the rank of "Sire" who claimed the discovery of the Eye of Rab'di.

Eastern Spirit: a shipping vessel based out of Klath and captained by Kadren Shasnar.

Ercanin (er-can-in): a chandler from Karbenath.

Estrom (es-trom): the capitol city of the nation, Kaladorn.

Eye of Rab'di (rahb-DEE): a large red gemstone

Feast of Sorrows: an annual feast held in commiseration by members of the Cherisium religion.

Fedirm Brandy (fee-durm): a type of strong alcohol.

Gastrim (gas-trim): a landlocked nation between Kerindor, the Hendan Principality, Klis, Kaladorn, the Western Sovereignty, and the Mindolarn Empire.

Ginalia (gin-AA-leeah): one of Nemral's romantic interests from his past.

Gorbian (GORE-beean): a coastal city on the eastern shores of the Sea of Korath.

Gorbian River: a large river running westward from the mountains dividing the Losian Gulf from the Sea of Korath. It is used as a common travel route for international travelers mooring in the Losian Gulf who wish to visit the Isle of Korath.

Grand Mage: a magic wielder specializing in wielding each of the seven magical channels: arcane, arpran, barsion, conjuration, elemental, illusion, and transmutation.

Grand Phineal: a thousand phineals, a length used for denoting large distances and often abbreviated G.P. on road signs and in conversations.

Hagen (hay-gen): a member of Iltar and Cornar's adventuring band, distinguished by his high-pitched voice and overly dramatic demeanor. He is an illusionist

Heleron (hell-ERR-on): a god to whom some

Sorothians and sailors pledge faith. His persona is typified as a merman wielding a trident.

Hemrin (hem-rin): a warrior in Cornar's adventuring band that has incredible luck.

High Valley, the: a mountain region north of the ruins of Karthar, the former capitol of the Karthar Empire. The High Valley is inhabited by a tribal clan called the Yelinail.

Illusionist: a mage specializing in creating illusions or enhancements.

Isle of Korath (core-ath): the largest island within the landlocked Sea of Korath.

Iltar (ILL-tar): a powerful necromancer from Soroth. He was born to an illusionist named Gwenyth and a Grand Mage from Alath named Adrin.

Irum'mak'sha (ee-room-mahk-shah): draconic title for the twelve dragons holding the highest knowledge of each magical discipline.

Jaedrin (jay-drin): the man who unearthed the Eye of Rab'di.

Kadren Shasnar (CAD-rin shass-nahr): the captain of the *Eastern Spirit.* Originally from Klath, located in the Kingdom of Los.

Kalda (call-duh): the name of the world.

Kaladorn (kal-AH-dorn): the northern most nation of men on the western side of the continent known as the Mainland. It borders the Elven Realm, the Western Sovereignty, and Gastrim.

Karbenath (CAR-bin-ath): a resort city along the northern shores of the Isle of Korath.

Karthar: a region along the northeastern continent of the

Mainland. Much of it is uninhabited by humans and is a forbidden land decreed by the early kings of Los. The neighboring nations enforce the borders, barring travelers or adventurers from entering the Karthar region.

Karthar Empire, the: an empire which rose to power twelve hundred years before Iltar's quest to find the Au'misha'k. The empire reigned over the entire continent known as the Mainland until it was overthrown by rebels based in Alath.

Kealor (key-lore): a vegetable with blue flesh. It has a bitter bite and a sour aftertaste.

Keav (keyv): a blue alcoholic beverage made from the kealor plant. The fermenting process heightens its bitter taste.

Kenard, Joselin (KIN-aard): a sea captain hired by Iltar and Cornar to charter their adventuring band.

Kerindor (ker-in-door): a nation lying on the borders of the Sea of Korath. It was once part of the Kingdom of Los but succeeded during the aggressive expansion of the Mindolarn Empire.

Kildath (kill-daath): a large city-nation located on the Kaldean Mainland.

Kingdom of Los: the largest of three powerful nations on Kalda; the others being Kildath and the Western Sovereignty. After the fall of the Karthar Empire, the Kingdom ruled all the Kaldean Mainland until the ninth king divided the borders, establishing a new Kildath and the Western Sovereignty. Since then many other nations have sprung from each of the three countries. Established by Dorin, the Mage-King, Los is a peaceful realm devoted to protecting the human realm.

Klath (claath): a port city off the Aglin Gulf, located on the Kaldean Mainland in the Kingdom of Los.

Korath (core-ath): the capitol city of the Isle of Korath, and the premier destination for leisure and relaxation.

Korathi Palace, the (core-ath-ee): a lavish castle atop cliffs overlooking the city of Korath.

Lavin root (lav-in): a sweet root often smoked in a pipe. It is a "cheap" substance used by the lower castes of the human realm.

League of Surveilors, the: an organization in the Losian military responsible for gathering information. They also investigate capitol crimes. Part of their organization is associated with the Kingdom Guard, assisting the armies of Los as advanced scouts in times of war.

Lightstone: a simplistic tevisrals that emits light.

Los: the capitol city of the Kingdom of Los.

Losian (lo-sian): a term for any native of the Kingdom of Los.

Mage: a general designation for anyone who can wield magic. Mages are often identified by their particular discipline: arpranist, barsionist, conjurer, illusionist, necromancer, transmuter and wizard.

Messel (meh-sull): a popular tea made from the inner bark of a tree of the same name.

Mindolarn Empire, the (mine-DOE-lahrn): a nation on the Kaldean Mainland also known as Mindolarn.

Moskian (moss-KEY-ahn): a revivalist period coinciding with the reformation of the Western Sovereignty and Kildath, some two hundred years after the fall of the Karthar Empire. Many art forms were rediscovered during this period.

Nath: a member of Tilthan's thieving troupe, originally from Klath.

Nemral (NEHM-rall): a thief, and the newest member of Tilthan's small band. Originally from Klath.

Nordal (NORE-dahl): a warrior trained by Cornar, and a member of Iltar's adventuring band. Originally from Klath.

Orchin's Tavern (ore-chin): a low-class tavern and gambling den in the city of Soroth.

Ordreth (ORD-reth): a young warrior in Iltar and Cornar's adventuring band, and Cornar's nephew.

Phineal (PHEN-ee-ahl): the standard length of measurement on Kalda; the equivalent of seventeen and a half inches or forty-three centimeters.

Principality of Soroth: a nation made up of various islands: Soroth, Sereth, Sarn, Silgarn, Seriel, Sorgil, Scagarn, Sogil, Sorti, Sangarn, Scain, Sengarn, Seril, Sargon, Seron, Spilath, Scon, Scagil. Each island has their own democratic system. Representatives from each island sits on a national council arbitrated by the Governor of Soroth.

Regalleon (ree-gal-leon): a ferry that traverses the land-locked Sea of Korath, between Korath and Gorbian.

Retarin (RE-taar-IN): one of Chernil's bodyguards.

Ril'Sha (reel-SHAH): draconic name for, council. Anciently, the Ril'Sha was the ruling body of all dragonkind, with a representative from each draconic breed. After the dragon wars, the Ril'Sha consisted of seven to twelve platinum dragons.

Rystra (ris-trah): a river-side city in the nation of

Gastrim. Rystra is a border city and a point it entry into Gastrim from Kerindor.

Sea of Korath: a landlocked sea on the Mainland, the
largest continent in Kalda's western hemisphere.

Sharon: the only female thief in Tilthan's thieving troupe,
and Ordreth's lover

Sharzen: a game of chance played with a card deck con-
sisting of seven suites of twelve cards.

Soroth (SORE-oth): the largest landmass in the island
chain comprising the Principality of Soroth. Its largest
city shares the same name.

Tefan, the Headless (te-fahn): a ghost rumored to steal
the heads of men, from the folktale of a man named
Tefan who was beheaded after committing dozens of
murders by decapitation.

Tevisral (TEV-is-rahl): any device capable of manifest-
ing or channeling magic.

The Fairy and The Drake: an inn named after a pairing
in the card game, Sharzen. The pairing is quite favorable, and

Thieving Cloak: a tevisral granting the ability to disap-
pear instantaneously by invisibility magic.

Thieving Lenses: a tevisral enabling the wear to see a
wide spectrum of light and magic.

Thieving Rod: a tevisral that shifts in shape by innate
transmutive magic.

Thousand Years War, the: a series of conflicts spanning
over a millennium. It began when Cheserith, a red
dragon, rebelled against his fellow Ril'Sha, seeking to
lay claim to his right to rule all Kalda. It brought about
a permanent schism between dragonkind. Among men

it is commonly known as the "Dragon Wars."

Tilthan (till-thaan): a notorious thief from Klath, and leader of a small band of thieves.

Transmute: a type, or channel, of magic that changes the composition of physical matter from one state to another.

Uligon (oo-LEE-gone): a prestigious man in the nation of Korath and a close associate of Chernil.

Voglin (vog-LIN): a town along the foothills of the Black Mountains in the nation of Cordath.

Western Sovereignty, the: a nation on the western side of the Mainland. Its capital is the coastal city, Tor.

White Duchess, the: Captain Kenard's sea vessel, made of a material that cannot rot nor rust. It has six decks, two above the main deck, and three masts.

Xlyar (sly-aar): one of Chernil's bodyguards.

CONNECT WITH THE AUTHORS

Stay up to date on future releases, upcoming Kickstarter campaigns, booksignings, and author appearances by signing up for Dan Zangari & Robert Zangari's mailing list at:

http://www.legendsofkalda.com/newsletter.html

Official Facebook Page:
https://www.facebook.com/legendsofkalda

AUTHOR'S AFTERWORD

ROBERT ZANGARI

Over the last several years, fans have expressed an interest in seeing more of Tilthan, the notorious sneak who is as skilled as he is sarcastic. While revising our series, **TALES OF THE AMULET**, we decided to give Tilthan a spotlight of his own. Tilthan was only mentioned by name in *A Prince's Errand* and so his exclusion in the novel begged a few questions: If Krindal's quest was the greatest adventure of the last thousand years, why didn't Tilthan and his buddies go with Cornar? And, what would Tilthan be doing while the others were gone? Wouldn't Tilthan be doing something worthwhile?

So, *A Thief's Way* was born of those questions.

It was a rocky birth, with revision after revision. I wanted a heist story, similar to the story-arc in *The Mages' Agenda* with magic and perils. But I couldn't figure out what I wanted Tilthan and his friends to steal. Or where they were stealing from...

Then, I turned toward an assassination plot. Tilthan is no stranger to assassinations, and he was eager to assassinate the Necrotic Order's council in *The Dragons' Legacy*. This idea had Tilthan and his thieving companions traveling to Sarn, an island in the Principality of Soroth, to eliminate Lady Ralisu Davig. As I wrote the Greater Kalda chapters of *A Prince's Errand* I wove some foreshadowing into Balden's segment, hinting that the good-lady need to be eliminated. I thought perchance that Baron Cilgan would work with an intermediary on Soroth to hire

Tilthan and the thieves to kill her. But, that ultimately didn't pan out, causing too many contradictions that messed with the outlined plot of the second book in the series, *The Dark Necromancer*.

I scratched my head for a few months and continued to work on part three of *A Prince's Errand*. It wasn't till I finished the novel that I figured out the plotting for *A Thief's Way*. I revisited the heist idea, but this time I set it all the way across the world on the Isle of Korath, a lavish resort-nation that thrives on tourism all year round. The Isle of Korath was the setting for Ercanin's Greater Kalda chapter in *A Prince's Errand*, and so the place was fairly fresh in my mind. But instead of taking place in Karbenath, *A Thief's Way* is centered in the capitol city called, Korath.

With our further adieu, we proudly present Tilthan's very first published stand-alone. We hope you enjoy *A Thief's Way*. Be sure to write us a review when you're finished.

– Robert Zangari
Salt Lake City, 2019

ABOUT THE AUTHORS

Dan Zangari is the creator of the Legends of Kalda fantasy universe, a work-in-development since the early 1990's. He received a Bachelor's of Science in Aerospace Engineering from the University of Southern California and a Masters Degree in Systems Management. His love for science fiction and fantasy prompted the creation of this fantasy universe. When he's not writing he enjoys reading, watching movies, spending quality time with family and serving in his local church congregation.

Robert Zangari is the co-author of the various books which belong to the Legends of Kalda universe. He studied Bio-Medical Engineering at the University of Utah; however, his love for stories and storytelling took him down a different career path. When he's not writing he enjoys spending time with his wife and daughters, playing video games, practicing martial arts and immersing himself in a good story.

CPSIA information can be obtained
at www.ICGtesting.com
Printed in the USA
LVHW091958030121
675572LV00025B/632/J